OPERATION VALASTRO

PROMISE ME A MIRACLE
BOOK FOUR

U. M. HIRAM

D2R MANAGEMENT GROUP

This story is a work of fiction. Names, characters, places, and incidents are products of the author's imagination or are used fictitiously and are not to be construed as real. Any resemblance to actual events, locales, organizations, or persons, living, dead or somewhere in between, is entirely coincidental.

Copyright © 2024 by D2R Management Group. All rights reserved.

Edited by J.L. Campbell www.joylcampbell.com and Ellen Kiley Goeckler

Stephanie M. Freeman https://stephaniemfreemanauthor.com/ and Lissa Woodson https://naleighnakai.com/

Cover Designed by J.L. Woodson: www.woodsoncreativestudio.com

Interior Designed by Lissa Woodson: www.naleighnakai.com

ISBN 979-8-9864632-7-8 (eBook)

ISBN 979-8-9864632-6-1 (Paperback)

Without limiting the rights under copyright reserved above, no part of this publication may be reproduced, stored in, or introduced into a retrieval system, or transmitted, in any form, or by any means (electronic, mechanical, photocopying, recording, or otherwise) without the express written permission of both the copyright owner and the publisher of this book, except in the case of brief quotations embodied in critical articles and reviews.

For permission, contact

632 Tuttle Creek Boulevard, #1053

Manhattan, KS 66502

Website: www.authorumhiram.com

Email: authorumhiram@umhiram.com

The scanning, uploading, and distribution of this book via the Internet or via any other means without the permission of the owner is illegal and punishable by law. Please purchase only authorized electronic editions and do not participate in or encourage electronic piracy of copyrighted materials. Your support of the author's rights is appreciated.

If you purchase this book without a cover, you should be aware that this book is stolen property. It is reported as "unsold and destroyed" to the publisher, and neither the author nor the publisher has received any payment for this "stripped" book.

U. M. HIRAM
ACKNOWLEDGEMENTS

To those who have aspirations, dreams, and goals that they want to see come to fruition. Know that it is possible if you keep pressing forward and have faith no matter how long it may take. Remember, there's no set timetable or age limit to see the desires of your heart become the realities of your existence.

Acknowledgements

First and foremost, I am grateful to God for allowing me to be on this amazing literary journey. I am humbled and excited to continue to share my writing gift and receive support from so many great people.

Naleighna Kai, your literary expertise is something to behold. I am appreciative of your continued support personally and professionally, and persistence to push me out of that all too familiar comfort zone. Thank you and I'm looking forward to seeing all that is on the horizon.

J.D. Mason, what can I say? You have been with me on this literary journey from the beginning. My first coach and mentor who still provides me with valuable insight and continued support. Thank you for your wisdom and friendship. I will forever be grateful to you.

J.L. Campbell and Stephanie M. Freeman, I appreciate you both for the developmental and content editing. Most of all, thank you for your guidance and friendships.

D.J. Mitchell, thank you so much for your time and beta reading expertise. Your candor, honest and thought-provoking feedback are truly appreciated.

J.L. Woodson, you are an amazing cover designer, graphic designer and creative extraordinaire. Thank you for continuing to raise the bar with all the phenomenal visual art that you create.

Tribe Called Success, my literary family, I appreciate each and every one of you. Your encouragement, support and love are priceless. From my heart to yours, thank you so much.

Readers and Reviewers, you are the reasons that an author has a platform to create and share their written art with the world. Thank you for your continued support.

CHAPTER 1

"Valentina, can you hear me?" Lorenzo kneeled down next to her body. One of the student chefs had caught her head before it connected with the Italian marble tile.

She was still unresponsive, but labored breathing caused her chest to faintly rise and fall. Panic filled the kitchen area as most of the staff stood immobile. Shock and disbelief ran among them.

"Someone call 112. Hurry," he yelled.

"I already did," a voice sounded behind him. He didn't look back to acknowledge that staff member. He was relieved they had acted in such a quick fashion.

Despite his best attempts at having Valentina show signs of movement, there was no response. He was upset that he didn't push her to take a break earlier. *Damn.*

"Is she going to be okay?" another person asked, standing on his left-hand side.

"The ambulance is on its way," he replied in a matter-of-fact tone. "Chef Valentina is strong, and I believe that she'll be fine." Valentina was one of the healthiest people that he knew, so this sudden turn of events was baffling.

A substantial amount of time had passed before the ambulance arrived, or so it seemed. Sirens wailed outside the building, announcing their arrival.

Moments later, the emergency medical team did everything they could to bring Valentina into a conscious state. None of their efforts worked. Running a hand through his cropped jet-black mane as the paramedics maneuvered to get Valentina on the stretcher, Lorenzo did his best to remain calm.

Externally, he displayed strength and leadership. Internally, he was struggling and worried about her condition. He couldn't lose her.

"Sir, how long has she been unconscious?" one of the emergency medical team members asked.

"About twenty minutes," Lorenzo answered with a quick look at his watch. "Valentina's head didn't hit the floor. Someone was able to get to her quickly."

"Good to know," the blond medic said. "What was she doing prior to her passing out?"

"Trying to put on her chef's coat," he replied, rolling through his memory. "Valentina had laid down in her office to take a quick nap. I looked in on her minutes later, then left her alone. She needed it. Working long days and nights to get ready for tonight's youth fundraising event and high volume of clients seemed to take a toll on her."

"Had she been complaining about not feeling well or anything hurting?"

"No, she didn't," Lorenzo responded, trying to keep the frustration out of his tone. He had enough of the questions. Valentina being taken to the hospital is what was most important to him.

As the paramedics finished taking her vitals, they carefully placed her on the gurney and strapped her in. She was still breathing lightly, but no other physical movement occurred.

"Sir, we'll be transporting Ms. Romano to the emergency room at Rome General Hospital."

"Thank you," Lorenzo said, feeling a little of the worry subside. "I'll head that way shortly."

Too late to cancel tonight's event. He had to put Plan B in place. Valentina would be livid if the fundraiser didn't go off without a hitch. But there wasn't much that she could do about it now. That's where he had to be in her corner.

Once the transport had whisked Valentina away, the kitchen staff were focused in his direction. A majority of them went back to working while others were reeling from the stir caused by Valentina's health situation. She was always a whirlwind of strength and energy. After gathering his thoughts, Lorenzo pivoted and met gazes with Thomas, who was standing nearby. "I need to see you in my office."

Turning to Vivian, one of their senior chefs, he said, "Please have everyone work on their assigned dishes and I'll be out on the floor shortly." Moments later, he was standing in an office tucked right next to the door leading into the wine cellar. Going over the event agenda took less than fifteen minutes. While pacing the industrial carpeting of his office, Lorenzo had been looking at his watch the entire time.

"Do you need anything from me before I head to the hospital?"

"No, we got this," Thomas replied. "Make sure Valentina's okay, and we'll handle things here until you get back."

"Tonight is important," he said. "We have to make sure nothing else goes wrong."

Placing a hand on Lorenzo's right shoulder, he said, "I know, and I promise that we'll operate as if Valentina was watching."

Based on his experience and tenure with the organization, Thomas was slated to be the third in charge. He'd been working at Taste of Romano for ten years, but had thirty years of culinary expertise. He'd met Valentina and Lorenzo after finishing their training at the International School of Culinary Arts. Years later, she had recruited him to join her company.

Lorenzo scanned the kitchen, taking in the synchronized

movements of the chefs and delicious aromas that tickled his nostrils. "Honestly, if we didn't already have all of this food prepared, I would cancel this entire event."

"I get that and understand," Thomas countered. "You know we can't do that. We have the donors for the youth culinary program and potential investors for the franchise expansion attending." He waved Lorenzo away. "Don't worry about things here. I can handle it. You do trust me, right?"

Taking a deep breath before maneuvering towards the hallway, Lorenzo answered, "You know I do. This just doesn't feel right with what's happening to Valentina right now."

"Everything will be perfetto," Thomas replied as he gestured with his index finger and thumb softly touching his lips. "Just keep me posted."

"Sure thing."

Snapping his fingers after remembering one final detail, he added, "if you hear from Lola Samuels about the huge wedding ceremony that Valentina has been hired to cater in the States, please let her know that we'll be back in touch. Don't share the details of what is happening right now. That's the last thing a bride who is 4,000 miles away on another continent needs to worry about."

"I got this. Now you get to the hospital."

Lorenzo went to his office, grabbed wallet and keys, then ran out to his silver Ferrari Portofino.

Meanwhile, a shadowy figure watched him leave and laughed before saying, "One down and a few more to go."

CHAPTER 2

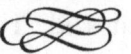

A piercing scream echoed throughout the event hall and a woman ran inside.

The music halted and everyone turned in her direction.

"Help us please. My mother isn't breathing."

Tears streamed down her ivory face while she gasped and scanned the people around her for a response.

Dr. Marcus Kyncade sprang to his feet and approached. "I'm a doctor. Where is she?"

"She's right out here," the brunette replied between sobs, gesturing to the foyer area. "We were walking back from the restroom, sat down for a few minutes, and my mother passed out. Now, she isn't breathing."

Maneuvering past the hysterical woman, he knelt next to the elderly one, whose face was pale as her daughter's. Shrugging out of his black jacket and focusing on the woman, he asked, "Did she fall to the floor?"

"No, I placed her there. She was sitting up, then started gasping for air and slouched over," she sobbed. "I just need her to be all right."

5

A few people trickled out of the event hall to see what was happening.

Immediately, he tilted the elderly woman's head back to open her airway, then checked her breathing. After a few seconds, he determined that there wasn't any response and began CPR.

"Someone, call 112."

Kneeling on the other side of the unconscious woman, a brown-haired man in a suit said, "I just got off the phone with them. I'm a registered nurse. Is there anything I can do to assist?"

Without stopping his lifesaving efforts, Marcus replied, "Just keep everyone at bay and an eye on her daughter."

Ten minutes later when the emergency medical team arrived, they took over care of the woman stretched out on the royal blue carpeted floor.

"Thank you for the great work you did here," one of the EMTs said with admiration in his voice.

"I only did what I took an oath to do."

"Don't be so modest, Dr. Kyncade," the young man said. "She's very lucky you were in the building and able to help before we arrived." The two men shook hands as the patient was prepared for transport.

Music resumed as everyone made their way back into the event hall. Marcus went into the bathroom to wash his hands. His muscles rippled under the crisp white shirt that somehow didn't get wrinkled while he performed CPR.

Shortly after, he stood on the terrace outside the banquet, closed his eyes and inhaled the cool air that came off the still lake. His thoughts briefly went back to the days serving as a military special operator, having to participate in some fierce battles behind enemy lines as well as provide medical care to his injured comrades. It fueled his passion to pursue his current career path from humble beginnings on a farm in South Carolina to living abroad in the capital city of Italy.

Seconds later, his peaceful moment was interrupted by a high-pitched voice. "Marcus, I've been looking all over for you."

Taking a deep breath, he faced the petite, raven-haired woman walking toward him. "You found me. Is something wrong?"

"Nothing at all." Eva closed the space between them and placed a slender diamond jeweled hand on his arm. "At least not anymore. Since you took care of that poor woman who was in so much distress."

He gave her his best smile; the one reserved for strangers or people who got under his skin. "You remember what I do for a living, right?"

"Of course. Don't be so silly," she replied with an irritating laugh. "I was just trying to say that I'm glad you were here to help."

Glancing out at the towering landscape of Rome, the ancient ruins of a centuries old castle provided a majestic backdrop across the still lake. He exhaled a calming breath, saying, "Me too."

She inched closer, he backed up and held out his arm to gently halt her approach. "I came here to support your event because it supports STEM programs for the local area youth."

She pouted ruby red lips. "But Marcus..."

His hand lowered, and he put more space between them. "I thought you understood we would be nothing more than friends."

"I did, but I changed my mind," she countered, attempting to bridge the space that separated them.

"A relationship is not what I'm looking for right now." He replied in as gentle a tone as he could manage.

At least not with you. He wouldn't say this to her outright. He'd already barely escaped being caught in a compromising position with her when she showed up at his office with nothing but a raincoat on, trying to seduce him. And she showed no sign of stopping.

Without further conversation, he moved around her and didn't look back. Several women had tried their hand at becoming Mrs. Kyncade, but Marcus kept them at bay. Right now, it was all about exercising self-control at this stage in his life, putting the young and wild college days behind him.

Entering the 8,000 square foot event hall decorated in purple, lavender, and gold, he scouted for his friend Jason, but couldn't locate him. Marcus wished to say goodbye, but also didn't want to have any more run-ins with Eva.

Spotting Jason near the bar, Marcus picked up the pace. "Hey man, I'm going to call it a night."

"Already? What happened?" Jason asked.

Scanning the large space, the music and chatter of the attendees had become distracting. He said, "I've had enough excitement for the evening."

"I understand. You should grab some food for the road."

"No, I'm good. It might've been the food that caused Ms. Sarah's distress." He chuckled, making light of the stressful incident.

"Mi scusi? I don't think so," a sultry voice sounded behind him. "Take that back."

Turning slowly, he gazed into the mesmerizing almond-shaped hazel eyes of a beautiful woman with a scowl that would cause anyone to head in the opposite direction. Her jet-black hair was styled in a neat ponytail while one of her arched eyebrows raised in annoyance. She wore a tailored white, embroidered chef's jacket with fitted black slacks and a comfortable pair of black shoes shining like freshly cleaned glass.

"It was just a joke," he said, chuckling. "And a private one at that. Why were you eavesdropping?"

Squaring her shoulders and locking gazes with him, she retorted, "That only happens when the comment is loud enough to be heard by everyone." Her right hand waved in a wide circle expressing her point.

Slightly tilting his head, Marcus showcased what some women considered his panty-melting smile. She rolled her eyes; totally missing all the charm he was known for.

"So, do you know the chef?" he asked.

"I know her very well, Dr. Kyncade," she shot back. "I'm Chef Valentina Romano."

She isn't just any chef, but a world famous one. Even he recognized her name.

"I'm sorry. I didn't mean to offend you, Ms. Romano."

"You wouldn't be the first to do that, but I accept your apology," she said. Her tone was abrupt and dismissive. "Have a good night."

Holding one hand over his heart as if wounded, Marcus's lips turned down in a playful pout. Smirking in annoyance at his gesture, but he also saw that she was trying not to smile. Valentina took one last glance at both men and walked toward the exit.

Watching as she walked away, he took in every curve of her body and inhaled the jasmine scented perfume. It had been a while since a woman had affected him in any way and the fact that this feisty chef had lit a flame spoke volumes. He shifted his gaze to Jason, who sipped his drink while watching the exchange.

That Woman. Damn.

CHAPTER 3

Racing down the legendary autostrada, Lorenzo made it to the hospital in record time. Despite the 80 mph speed limit, he completed the thirty-minute drive in fifteen. Usually his drive consisted of enjoying the open road and greenery of the umbrella pine trees while the sounds of Lorenzo's favorite Italian tenor Luciano Pavarotti filled the car speakers. However, today was very different. Pulling his car into a vacant "Emergency Room" parking space, he barreled out of the vehicle before breaking into a run.

He didn't give anyone at the front desk a chance to greet him before saying, "Can you tell me how Valentina Romano is doing? She was brought in here about twenty minutes ago."

"Good afternoon, Sir," the nurse said in a voice laced with a smooth Jamaican accent, her slim fingers still flying over the keyboard. "May I ask if you are related to the patient?"

"Not by blood," he answered, shifting to let another nurse pass. "But I am authorized to ask questions. There is a medical power of attorney on file here."

"I'll need to verify that information. May I see your ID please?"

the petite woman asked in a polite tone. Her voice sounded above the background noise conversation between nurses, monitors beeping in the distance, and footsteps scurrying across the polished floor while medical personnel moved swiftly to take care of other patients.

Pulling the black wallet out of the back pocket of his jeans, Lorenzo grabbed his driver's license and handed it over.

"Thank you." She glanced at the plastic card. "Mr. Ricci, I'll be right back." She went through a set of double steel doors and returned a few minutes later with a huge smile on her face.

"Mr. Ricci, I will let the doctor know you're here." She gestured to an area behind him. "In the meantime, you can have a seat in the waiting room."

The area was practically empty, so he sat close to the door. He checked his cell, but no messages had come through. Glancing at the ceiling, his mind filled with scenarios about Valentina's current health status. He was worried about her and growing impatient with the wait time to receive an update. Lorenzo loved this woman and had a vision of them not only being in business together, but getting married and having children. Once this medical emergency was over, he planned on letting her know that.

Thirty minutes later, a tall man wearing a white lab coat walked into the waiting area and scanned the few people whose conversations trickled to a halt. His brown-eyed gaze landed on his intended target, and something about him put Lorenzo on alert.

"Mr. Ricci, my name is Dr. Kyncade." His rich baritone echoed in the modern decorated space as he closed the distance between them. "I understand you've been asking about Ms. Romano's condition."

"Yes, I've been trying to find out how she's doing and what's going on with her," he replied. "How long will it be before I can see her?"

"I can take you to where she's currently resting. Then we can talk a little more about what's in store for her."

They went past the front desk and through the steel doors to a room where Valentina was attached to several machines and appeared to be sleeping. His heart ached seeing her in this condition and the clicks and beeps echoing in the room sounded foreboding.

"Has she woken up since being here?" Lorenzo asked, without taking his eyes off Valentina.

"She has not, and we're running several tests to find the source causing her condition," Dr. Kyncade said. "Ms. Romano's vitals are stabilized. She had a high fever, but we were able to bring that down."

As Lorenzo's thoughts panned to an image of her smiling, then giving a list of instructions, the attending physician continued by saying, "Valentina needs to be monitored closely for us to figure out why she hasn't regained consciousness. We will do everything to make sure she receives the best care."

After answering a few more questions about treatment timelines and what he needed to bring back to the hospital, the doctor left Lorenzo standing near Valentina's new electronic bodyguards as he swept out of the room. As he gazed at her, the thought of losing the woman he grew up with in rural Rome scared him. They'd been in each other's lives since elementary school, witnessing all of the ebbs and flows that life's experiences taught each of them.

Vibrations from his jeans pocket signaled an incoming call. Thomas' name flashed across the screen.

"Hey, is everything all right?" Lorenzo asked. "How's the event?"

"We have a major problem," Thomas replied, sounding a little on edge.

Hairs on the back of Lorenzo's neck tingled. "What it is, uomo?"

Brief silence on the other end only escalated Lorenzo's anxiety level. A few seconds passed before his patience ran out.

"Spill it, man. They'll be keeping Valentina overnight, so if I have to act on something, I need to do it now."

"I understand," he answered, but the unease in his voice was unmistakable, even with just those two words. "We had an interruption at tonight's event."

"What? I thought you said you could handle things." Lorenzo's elevated voice caught the attention of one of the registered nurses passing by.

"Sir, please lower your voice, or you'll need to finish the call outside," she said, giving him a stern look to match the warning.

"My apologies," he said, keeping his voice level.

When she disappeared, he focused on the call. "What do you mean the event was interrupted? You know how important this was for Valentina."

"I do, but we have a bigger problem."

Lorenzo jammed one hand through his hair. "Is there anything more significant than completing this event in a way that would make Valentina proud?"

"Four of our specialty chefs had an episode like Valentina's. All are being transported to the emergency room as we speak," he said as hurried footsteps, elevated voices, and distant sirens on the other end added to what sounded like total chaos. "Things got crazy around here after you left."

Lorenzo glanced at the phone in disbelief. *What the hell is going on?*

First, Valentina, and now more of their staff? All of this was surreal. Valentina was an isolated incident. Four members of their staff meant a pattern.

"Everyone's coming your way and I'll be right behind them," Thomas replied. "I have to make sure the space is cleared out and everything is locked up."

He disconnected the call, leaving Lorenzo with more questions than answers.

CHAPTER 4

Sliding his hand across his five o'clock shadow, Marcus glanced up at the dimly lit ceiling. He had been surprised when Valentina's comatose body was brought into the Emergency Room. Their interaction days ago at the STEM gala was brief but powerful. Her poise, aura and quick wit impressed him. And she wasn't bad on the eyes either. Her silky black hair, doe-shaped eyes, and plump lips were etched in his memory from that night of the STEM event.

She'd been on his mind, and he had every intention of contacting her again. It was rare that a woman made him reconsider his stance on dating. As fate would have it, now he was tasked with saving her life versus asking her to have dinner with him.

Four more people en route to the hospital were also experiencing the same symptoms. He had been at the desk when the call came in.

"What the hell is going on?"

He entered her room and witnessed Lorenzo kissing the back of her lifeless hand. He glanced at the machinery and realized all vitals remained the same. Before he could turn to leave, Lorenzo looked up.

"Dr. Kyncade, is everything all right?" he asked with concern laced in his voice. "Do you need something?"

"No, I didn't need anything. Just wanted to check in on Ms. Romano."

"I see," Lorenzo replied in a slightly aggravated tone, still clasping Valentina's hand.

Sensing that he had interrupted a private moment, Dr. Kyncade said, "I'll be back later to check in on her."

Knowing he only had a little time before things ramped up again, he wound his way to an office on the other side of the nurse's station. After closing the door, Dr. Kyncade sat in the black ergonomic mesh chair and leaned his head back. The day had been busy with a variety of cases coming through the hospital doors. They were all easy to deal with, until now.

Closing his eyes, he thought about Ms. Sarah. She'd been admitted to the hospital after her health crisis at the event where he saved her life. The diagnosis was a violent reaction to almonds that were in one of the dishes.

"Good morning, Ms. Sarah. How are you doing today?"

"I'm doing good, Dr. Kyncade," she replied. "But this hospital food sucks. Why don't they season this stuff?"

Smiling, he said, "I think it's because they want to make sure that you are eating healthy."

Sucking her teeth, she gave him a mocking glare, "Lies and more lies."

"How about this?" he began. "When you get out of here, I'll treat you to an enjoyable meal that does not include almonds."

"Are you flirting with me, young man?" She winked, then gestured for him to lean in. When he complied, she whispered, "my daughter is single, and she needs a man."

Marcus groaned inwardly, but smiled. "I'll see about getting her introduced to a good young man."

Gently patting his arm, the elderly woman said, "How about you? I think you're what she needs."

Chuckling, he replied, "I'm flattered. Let's just focus on you getting out of here."

Vibrations from his lab coat brought him out of that memorable moment with Ms. Sarah. She reminded him of his favorite great aunt. Moving past the shelves of medical journals, he walked briskly to the front of the hospital. His primary focus shifted to the task at hand. Saving lives.

CHAPTER 5

Sirens blared as ambulances pulled up to the emergency room entrance within minutes of each other. Lorenzo stepped out of Valentina's room and rushed to the front of the hospital to meet Thomas.

As soon as Lorenzo spotted him, he hurried over and asked, "Are you all right, man?"

Wiping his sweat-drenched brow with a hand towel, Thomas replied, "Si, this has been one crazy day."

"One minute everything is fine, then the ripple effect of one person." Lorenzo ran a hand over his freshly cut hair. He wondered if this strange occurrence would affect any more of their staff.

Both men moved closer to the wall as nurses whisked by to assist the emergency medical technicians with bringing in more of the unresponsive staff members. Lorenzo's stomach dropped as the men and women he worked with were wheeled by him.

"Everyone understood why we had to stop the event," Thomas explained. "It took a bit of time, but we were able to get them out as fast as possible. Just so you know, the rest of the food is going to local shelters."

"Thank you for handling all of that. Been a hell of a day for us."

Arriving in the quiet waiting room, Lorenzo and Thomas settled into the chairs near an open window. The cool breeze filled the space with fresh air.

Twenty minutes passed and the waiting room was crammed with family members of the four staff members. Crying and sounds of despair filled the space. Everyone was trying to get information about their loved ones, only to be told that the doctor would be out to speak with them soon.

"Mommy, where's my daddy? I wanna' see him," one little boy whined while his small hand was wrapped securely in the woman's sitting across from him.

Leaning his head so it touched the wall, Lorenzo closed his eyes. With this many key staff members down, it might prove difficult to find a balance between handling Valentina's healthcare needs and making sure the business kept running as smoothly as possible.

"Are you all right, Renzo?" Thomas asked.

"I'm good," he replied. "It's all of this waiting and then figuring out what to do next that has me on edge."

"Well, I'm here. Just let me know what you need, and I got you."

"I know. Thank you, man."

Forty-five minutes later, Dr. Kyncade appeared in the waiting area. Everyone looked at him anxiously, awaiting specific answers about their loved ones. Some of them left their seats to crowd around him.

"Good evening, everyone," he said. "I know that you all have questions, and I will talk to each family privately."

"Why can't you just talk to us all together?" a woman standing to his left asked in an exasperated tone.

"By law, I can't discuss everyone's medical information in that way," Dr. Kyncade said, keeping his tone calm. "The nursing staff will bring *authorized* family members back and I can answer specific questions."

Since Lorenzo had already spoken with him about Valentina, he didn't move from his current spot. He'd always hated hospitals because he had to watch his mother's health decline until she eventually died from congenital heart disease. That memory unraveled him, and he took a few deep breaths to calm his racing thoughts. The vivid picture of him holding her frail hand as she took her last breath was etched forever in his mind. He reflected for a few minutes to process all the events of the day and deal with his whirlwind of emotions before heading back to Valentina's room.

He closed his eyes and leaned his head back against the wall. He needed a few minutes to process everything, Lorenzo mulled over the fact that he wasn't able to stop this train wreck. He knew something wasn't quite right with Valentina and he wished that he'd been a little more adamant about her taking a break a lot sooner that day. His thoughts moved to a happier time when they were initially working through her business plan for the restaurant.

Walking through the spacious, stylish living room to the back patio, Lorenzo was mesmerized by the dark-haired beauty sitting in the lounge chair by the crystal clear pool. "Hi V, what are you doing?"

Smirking, she said, "What does it look like I'm doing, Renzo?"

"Being lazy instead of working on our business plan that is due by the end of this week."

"Do you mean mine?" *she replied, removing the black Chanel shades and placing them on the small blue table.*

"Okay, here we go." *Shaking his head, he asked,* "Why do you always do that?"

"Do what?"

"We know that this restaurant is your baby, but I am making a small investment in this venture as well with my money and chef skills."

Waving her hands in the air, Valentina replied. "Here we go. This is why I've always been skeptical of bringing someone in."

"I'm not just someone," he countered trying to keep the aggravation he felt from his voice. "We grew up together and are best friends. Did you forget that?"

Blowing out a calming breath, Valentina studied Lorenzo for a moment. "Look, you know how important this venture is for me. I don't want it to fail and this whole process has been stressful."

"I get that, but you have to remember that you're not in this alone. You are always trying to hold everything on your shoulders when you don't have to."

The swimming pool water rippled in the background as Valentina contemplated what Lorenzo said. She'd always been strong willed and guarded, even with those that she knew loved and cared about her.

"Look, I apologize Renzo. You know that I trust you with my life."

"Glad to hear that because I was starting to wonder."

Smiling, she said, "Now that our little tiff is out of the way, let's finish this business plan to get it ready for the bank."

"You better be glad that I love you, V."

Standing and strolling over to the patio table where the laptop and notepad were located, Valentina glanced over her shoulder. "I love you too. Let's get to work."

CHAPTER 6

A few hours earlier ...
   Sleep was for rookies.
   Thoughts ran through her brain as she counted the napkins and place settings. In a matter of hours the place would be bustling with dignitaries and celebrities in equal measure. So having a deep and personal relationship with her pillow was out of the question.
   Valentina and her staff were preparing for the Eclipse of Innovation: Valastro Youth STEM Gala and Capital Campaign in a few hours. A lot of dignitaries and celebrities would be in attendance. In preparation, Valentina hadn't gotten a lot of rest, which wasn't anything new for her. Over the past few days, she'd been physically feeling a little out of sorts.
   "Chef Romano, are you okay?" Lorenzo, her sous chef and childhood best friend, asked with a look of concern on his face.
   Standing at six feet tall, he towered over her five-foot-six-inch frame. His cropped black hair and neatly trimmed goatee accented a handsome, angular face.
   "I'm fine," she said even though dark circles were forming around her eyes.

"No offense, but you don't look so well," he said. *"You should probably take a break and let me handle things here for a little while."*

Valentina took a deep breath, glanced up at Lorenzo and then at her staff. Realizing a break was needed and that everyone was handling their duties, she chose not to debate with her business partner and best friend.

"Okay, I'll go upstairs to my office after finishing the desserts and rest for a little while."

"Good, just let me know if you need anything," Lorenzo replied in a sincere tone. He received a simple nod, taking this as a cue for him to leave her alone. After a brief hesitation, he moved to the other side of the kitchen, but kept a close eye on her.

In her peripheral, she watched as he walked away. Finishing up the Tiramisu Layered Cakes and Italian Rum Cheesecakes, Valentina took off her chef's coat. After taking a quick scan of the busy kitchen, she walked to the private elevator and headed to her secluded office on the third floor.

In the twelve hundred square foot space, a custom-made marble top mahogany desk and executive chair were sitting three feet away from the smoked glass windows. The spacious area also included a neatly arranged bookshelf, a mini-L-shaped bar, a private bathroom, and a large sofa. A seventy inch television was mounted on one wall, while oil paintings of beautiful Italian landscapes filled two of the other panels.

Valentina closed the office door by placing her hand on the hidden panel underneath the desk then plopped down in her chair. Rubbing her temple, the onset of a headache emerged. Perspiration rolled down her forehead and she began to feel a little overheated. Opening the top drawer, she pulled out, and turned on the miniature fan to cool herself off. All day she'd been feeling ill but refused to go home. Valentina would have gladly tossed herself into the nearest volcano than admit she didn't feel well or need help. Knowing how perceptive Lorenzo was, she allowed her pride to trump common sense earlier.

Her staff was more than capable of handling things. However, Valentina prided herself on being present and involved from start to finish. It was her name and reputation on the line. Years of hard work, along with building prominent lucrative relationships, helped her business grow and expand internationally.

"All I need is a nap," she said to herself. Realizing how much she'd been working and attending events non-stop, Valentina knew that her current schedule was taking its toll on her body. Standing and stretching, she took a slow trek to the couch and lay down.

Valentina covered herself with a royal blue cashmere throw. It had been gifted to her by her mother months ago, and it provided a sense of peace and comfort. She closed her eyes and dozed off. Thirty minutes later, Valentina woke up, but wasn't feeling any better than she had before she went to sleep. Determined to push forward anyway, she sat up slowly and waited a few minutes before attempting to stand.

"What is wrong with me?"

Entering her private bathroom she glanced in the mirror. Even her coloring was off. Her face was pale and lips slightly dry. She moistened both with water, then patted them dry with a plush towel. Something was wrong, but once again, denial was her fail safe reaction. Valentina brushed it off. Determined to complete the finishing touches to the signature dishes for tonight's event, she staggered to the elevator then straightened herself up before the doors opened leading to the kitchen area.

She made a visual sweep of the kitchen and met Lorenzo's eye for a moment. Everyone was focused on finishing their particular assigned dishes and other tasks. Taking a deep breath, she walked over to the parallel hanging coat rack.

Grabbing her chef's coat, she struggled to put it on. Shaking off the unease, she only took a few steps forward before her vision dimmed. The last thing that she heard was someone screaming her name and footsteps quickly approaching.

"Someone catch her, don't let her head hit the floor," the voice trailed off.

Valentina's body went free falling. All movement stopped and chaos erupted.

CHAPTER 7

Scratching his head, Dr. Kyncade studied the medical charts and test results of all five patients. Same symptoms, unresponsive and stable vitals. Baffling and challenging, but he was going to find a cure. All the signs were pointing in one direction, drugging, but it was not an easily traceable one.

"What type was used and why? What is going to the be the lasting effects?"

No one was in the room with him. Talking to himself was common practice as he worked through medical cases.

He was a highly trained physician known worldwide for his expertise in biomedical science and neurotoxins. Earning his four-year medical degree from the University of Maryland and continuing on for a fifth year to complete his master's degree in Cellular and Molecular Biomedical Science, he was knowledgeable about a variety of poisons and their potentially fatal effects on the human body.

Research played a major role during his college years and medical career. Dr. Kyncade earned a reputation for being a sought-after physician in his field. Frequently, he was asked to consult on medical cases, present information at conferences and give lectures at universities about his studies and firsthand experience with neurotoxins.

A knock on the slightly open door interrupted his thoughts as one of his colleagues entered the office. "Did you find anything yet?"

"No, not yet," he said to Barry Davidson, who was out of his focus because of the large desktop computer screens. "You know that will not stop me from trying to figure this out."

"Even with all five of the patients stabilized, it's strange that none of them have woken up," the gray-haired man replied while looking over his steel-framed glasses.

Leaning forward and taking a drink of bottled water, Dr. Kyncade said, "I know. I've never seen anything like this, and I've dealt with a lot of different conditions over the years."

"I have no doubt you'll be the one to figure this out." A genuine smile crossed the other man's lips. "Let me know if you need anything."

"I will, Barry, thanks."

Glancing at the smartwatch on his wrist after his colleague's exit, Marcus prepared to make patient rounds. His first stop was to see Valentina.

Entering the hospital room with the registered nurse on shift walking in directly after him, he pulled up Valentina's electronic medical chart. Her vitals looked excellent, and she was resting comfortably. They had run several tests for any traces of drugs that might've been in her system, but nothing was found. At least not yet. He was determined to keep doing everything in his power to get her well.

"How is our patient today?" he asked the nurse, showcasing his signature Hollywood smile.

"We have tried stimulating movement and nothing seems to work," she replied. "That's been the case for the other four patients as well."

"Hmm, that has been our biggest challenge," he said. "I'm hoping we'll get this figured out soon."

"We're hoping for the same thing, Dr. Kyncade."

"We'll keep on our current regimen," he shared. "If there's another medical treatment we need to try, then I'll share that with everyone."

"Thank you, Dr. Kyncade," his assisting nurse replied in a seductive voice, while batting her eyelashes.

Ignoring the obvious flirtation and walking towards the door, he said, "Okay, let's go and check on the other patients. Also, please make sure to get an extra blanket for Ms. Romano and cover her up. I noticed the chill bumps on her arms and we want to make sure that she is as comfortable as possible."

Two hours later, he was back in his office studying chart information and continuing research. After realizing that he hadn't eaten anything, he grabbed a large chef's salad topped with grilled chicken from his private fridge, then chose a spot to enjoy it outside of the hospital. It was sunny, and the temperature was in the mid-70s. Since cooking was one of his favorite hobbies, he did a lot of meal preparation.

After clearing his mind, nourishing his body, and mulling over a few scenarios, he pulled out his phone and scrolled through his contacts then pressed the name on the screen. Even though their medical specialties were different, he had great respect for this fellow physician. Needing a different perspective, he knew that this man was the person to consult with about these cases.

Closing the office door, he then reclaimed a seat in that comfortable office chair. Taking a deep breath, Dr. Kyncade tapped the screen on his cell phone and waited.. Three rings later, he said, "Hello, Dr. Maharaj, how are you?"

"Marcus Kyncade, it's been a long time," the voice on the other end of the phone said. "I'm good. How are you?"

"Doing well," he replied. "You know me, looking for the next cure."

Shuffling papers on the other end signaled his colleague was multitasking. "I forgot you live, breathe and eat medicine. You need a woman, Marcus."

"Correction, Jai," he sighed, "I need the *right* woman." Thoughts briefly shifted to one particular raven-haired beauty that was capturing his heart. Shaking his head, he knew he could never cross that line.

"All right, I stand corrected." After a slight pause, Jai continued, "Well, I know this isn't a social call. What can I help you with?"

"Still direct and to the point just like our college days. You were straight no chaser."

"Always my friend," Jai said with a chuckle. "It cuts out a whole lot of small talk."

"I have this medical case, well five of the same, that has me stumped," he began. "I would like your thoughts on a few things."

"Sure, I have some time," Jai said. "Tell me about them."

Pausing after he'd finishing telling Jai about the cases, Marcus said, "You know I'm not easily baffled, but these cases are unique because the root cause is not easy to identity. My gut is telling me it's poison. Just not one that is easy to pinpoint."

After a few seconds of silence, Jai said, "I think you're right and I was scheduled for a trip to come out that way. Let me check on a few things and I'll plan to see you soon."

"Sounds like a plan," Marcus replied and disconnected the call.

Picking up his research notes and one of the patient files, he pulled up some information on one of the computer screens. Leaning forward, Marcus said, "That's it. Well, I'll be damned."

CHAPTER 8

*J*ai's private plane was preparing to land in the *"City of the Seven Hills"* days later, after he agreed to consult with his friend and colleague. After reviewing the secure medical files, he immediately flew to Rome. The mystery and suspicion surrounding the five cases seemed to be connected to someone the Castle was tracking.

Besides that, Chef Valentina Romano was the top choice for Dro and Lola's wedding, so this made things personal for him. With the King of Hyde Park still being detained in the Middle Eastern country of Ajid, this provided an opportunity for his Castle family to make sure things kept moving forward with the upcoming nuptials while they worked on a plan to safety extract him. Jai was determined to find a solution for the latest crisis that involved the woman who was supposed to prepare a fabulous feast for the wedding.

"Dr. Maharaj, do you need anything else?" the lone flight attendant asked.

Looking up from his computer and smiling, he replied. "No, I'm fine. Thank you, Laura."

Forty minutes later, the pilot announced they were preparing for landing. Securing his seatbelt and closing his laptop, he patiently waited for the plane to touch down. As soon as the pilot taxied into their assigned area, Jai's private vehicles pulled up to the hangar. Two black SUVs and two drivers that looked like linebackers waited for him. He rode in the lead vehicle with the driver and one security team member. The trailing SUV was occupied by four additional members of his assigned security team. Jai was heavily protected on this trip because of his King of Devon status and being Khalil Germaine's son. The Kings, Knights, and Queens were all targets because of the work they did to improve the lives of others, their global influence, and wealth.

He briefed the Castle members on his suspicions regarding Chef Valentina and her staff members being drugged. All evidence pointed to Lewis Wingate's involvement. He had caused a lot of trouble when his illegal warehouse activities escalated, and the Kings worked tirelessly to stop his operations. The group tracked his last known movement to Rome.

That man caused so much heartache for Dro and Lola with help from his former business partner Alistar Mayhew. Her kidnapping and eventual rescue was still fresh in everyone's mind and festered like an open wound. Now, their wedding was approaching, and chaos was erupting in all the important parts of the wedding. First, the maid of honor, the ring, then the dressmaker, and now the cuisine. Hopefully, no one tried to sabotage the flowers, too.

Thanks to the latest information from the International Joint Crime Task Force and finding out there was an antidote that the five patients needed, Jai waited to have that conversation with Marcus in person. The agency had undercover agents working within Lewis Wingate's warehouse and who were able to reveal the exact location of the antidote. Some quick work behind the scenes would help to obtain the required medication to treat the patients. Jai was tasked with running point for the Castle as well as assisting his colleague.

His vibrating cell phone interrupted Jai's thoughts as he reached for the phone in his jacket pocket.

"I just got in the car and I'm heading to the hotel," he said.

"Glad that you made it safely, brother," Marcus replied.

"Once I get checked in and talk with my family, I will call you and we can meet up."

"Sounds good. I look forward to it."

After disconnecting the call, he touched base with Calvin Atwood, a Knight of the Castle and protégé of Daron Kincaid, King of Morgan Park, and a brilliant inventor. The plan was for him to join Jai overseas in a couple of days after ensuring they had all the manpower needed.

Jai checked into his hotel suite and took a quick shower. The next thing on the agenda was to video call his wife Temple. He knew she was a little anxious about him making this trip with so much going wrong surrounding the wedding. At the rate things were going, it would take a miracle to pull it off. But his wife also understood what his Castle status as King of Devon meant. He didn't have a choice about giving assistance when it was needed by anyone connected to the Castle.

An hour later, Jai was sitting in an upscale restaurant at a private table across from his friend. Both men loved Indian food, and this was one of Marcus's favorite culinary venues to frequent. Crimson paint served as the backdrop for gold accents, light fixtures, and oil paintings of historic ancient ruins adorning the walls. Dimmed lighting created an intimate setting along with the instrumental music playing through the surround sound speakers.

After taking a sip of his water, Jai said, "I'm glad that you called me about the medical cases, brother."

Placing his glass of sparkling water on the table, Marcus said, "Me too. I know I can trust you and you're a brilliant doctor."

"No need to inflate my ego. I'm already here to help." Laughing, they both turned their attention to the server, who came over to take their order of curried lamb, basmati rice, and vegetables.

Once they were free to speak again, Jai said, "Thanks to your research and intel, we know the exact location of the antidote. It's in that warehouse you told me about not too far from the hospital."

Stopping his glass midway to his mouth, Marcus replied, "Damn, I knew there was something weird going on at that place. I couldn't get close enough to figure it all out and didn't think it was smart to do that alone."

"I'm glad to hear that, brother. There are plans to retrieve it but I didn't want to share that over the telephone. We are going in to get it as soon as everyone is in place."

Looking Jai square in the eyes, he said, "Who's car are we taking?"

Jai raised an eyebrow to that question.

"What? You already know I'm down for the action. I didn't do all that special ops training for nothing."

"I thought you did that to pay for medical school," Jai chuckled.

Moments later, their food arrived. While they ate, they discussed the specifics of the drug and the status of the patients.

"So, the neurotoxin that was used came from the venom of a Mediterranean black widow spider," Marcus shared. "It took me a little while to narrow down the exact type."

Jai smiled, "And that is why you are the best of the best in your field, brother."

Raising his glass, Marcus replied. "Right back at you."

"Do we know if there were any strange people who had access to the building? Or staff acting in a guilty manner?"

"I understand that there was service on a broken line in the filtration system in the private break area for senior staff."

Both men shared a knowing glance and determined that was

how those specific individuals came into contact with the neurotoxin. Time was working against them, so they had to ensure that the antidote was secured quickly or the patients would face paralysis or death. There was no way Marcus would lose any of his patients without a fight—especially not Valentina.

CHAPTER 9

An eerie stillness surrounded the building where Lewis Wingate's men were hiding out. He had been attempting to evade capture with the help of powerful global allies. As the Castle and Joint Crime Task Force silently took each of them out of play, his circle of false protection was reduced. Arrests and plea deals were becoming the common theme for those who had been assisting him. Now it was harder for him to ask anyone else to help because word had gotten around that he no longer had *The Midas Touch*.

Kidnapping and drugging were at the top of the long list of his crimes. Alister Mayhew, Wingate's former best friend and co-conspirator, cooperated with Jai along with the Castle members and task force to provide additional intel to track him down. Disheartening, given the fact that he knew so many secrets that could cause Alister much harm.

Sitting inside one of the blacked-out SUVs parked a short distance from the warehouse, Jai and Marcus went over last-minute details about entering the warehouse. Dr. Kyncade tried to get Valentina out of his mind. Something about the feisty woman pulled at him and he could not understand why. He had to save her. And he needed to know the reason someone would hurt her and the others this way.

"Are you ready for this takedown?" Jai asked.

"Is that a trick question, brother?" Marcus replied. "Watch me move. Then you can answer that question for yourself."

Jai smirked. "All this from a guy that was so serious in college but dressed up like Santa for the pediatric fundraiser and a clown with a big red nose for that gala event last year."

Through the intel collected and the Castle's state-of-the-art technology, they were able to pinpoint this exact location. Several men patrolled the exterior of the warehouse, wearing bulletproof vests and carrying semiautomatic guns. Jai, Marcus, and the men assigned to this mission fanned out across the property. Blending into the scenery with the deadly grace that came from years of practice.

Once inside the warehouse, their focus would be to get to the lab in the central hub of the structure. Jai held up a portable heat seeking, infrared device that assisted them with identifying the number of hostiles they would have to engage. They figured this was the area patrolled by heavily armed guards.

Jai's voice echoed through the communications headsets of both teams. "Getting the antidote is priority number one. Let's make sure we make this retrieval effort count and come out whole."

"Roger that," Marcus said. "Apprehending Wingate is our second priority because that man needs to pay for all the chaos that he has caused."

No way would he escape the inevitable this time. Too much had happened, and proof of his crimes was in the Kings and Knights' possession—pictures, documents, and witnesses who were willing to testify against him.

The teams split into two, with Jai and Marcus serving as the leads.

"Marcus, is your team ready?" Jai asked.

"Ten-four, we're ready to rock and roll," Marcus replied, using old school lingo.

"Let's sync watches and move out in ten minutes."

They counted down the seconds and right on time, each team moved in a synchronized fashion. A short volley of suppressed gunfire and the exterior of the warehouse was cleared so the teams could make entry. Heading inside from two different directions, the exchange of gunfire grew more intense. Bodies dropped to the concrete as if dominoes were being played in a high stakes game.

Marcus and Jai made it to the epicenter of the warehouse where the antidote was being housed. Lewis Wingate lifted the vials from one of the refrigerated trays and secured them in a heavily padded protective case before rushing out the back door in an attempt to make a run for it and escape to freedom.

"I got him," Marcus said. "You handle the rest of them." Taking off at a sprint, he closed in on Wingate's retreating form and tackled him. Wingate tried to put a wrestling move on Marcus, but failed miserably. He was four inches shorter than Marcus and had the physique of a slim marathon runner. The doctor and former special operator overpowered him in a sleeper hold, while Wingate flailed on the hard surface.

"Let me go," Wingate commanded in a wavering, high-pitched tone.

"Oh, I will, and you'll be on your way to your new accommodations," Marcus replied without releasing his firm grip.

Moments later, Marcus reappeared with Lewis Wingate ahead of him back to where Jai and the rest of the group were standing at the door of the warehouse. His hands were zip-tied behind his back and he tried to wiggle out of the taller man's firm hold.

Seconds later, a team from the international joint crime task force and local authorities converged on the warehouse and took him, along with several other men, into custody.

"Man, how did you take Wingate down without getting a

scratch or bruise?" Jai asked with his focus on the teams sweeping the area and gathering evidence.

Without cracking a smile, Marcus replied, "As I told you earlier, watch me move."

Jai smiled at that bold statement. "You got that right, brother. Never let the smoothness fool you."

"Seriously, that special ops training comes in handy," he glanced at Jai and nodded. "Especially when people don't realize there's more to this doctor than saving lives."

Both men refocused their attention on the activities at the warehouse. Many of the assailants were being escorted out in handcuffs, and those who had been injured were given medical care. Jai and Marcus prepared to head to the hospital as soon as they received the all-clear to leave the area.

Fifteen minutes later, Jai and Marcus were in an SUV being escorted to Rome General Hospital. As soon as they arrived, they changed into medical gear and began the treatment process on the five poisoned patients.

CHAPTER 10

"Take your hands off of me. Who's in charge here?"
"Please ma'am, I need you to calm down."
"No, I won't calm down. Why am I here?"

Striding toward Valentina Romano's hospital room, Marcus and Jai were confident that they would see an improvement in all five patients. The antidote had already been administered, and time given for the medicine to settle in each person's system. Gently pushing the door open, Marcus' stride faltered, causing Jai to stutter step behind him.

"What's wrong, Marcus?" Jai asked. "I almost ran into you."

"Sorry about that," he replied. Regaining his composure, he continued his trek into the room. They came face to face with an alert but irate patient. The attending nurse was trying to settle her down.

"What is all of this?" Valentina asked, with more than a hint of irritation in her semi-hoarse voice. "Where the hell am I?"

"Ms. Romano, please calm down," the nurse said. "Dr. Kyncade is more than happy to answer your questions, but you've been through an ordeal. It's best that you lay down and rest."

Nodding in acknowledgment, he turned his attention to the beautiful woman looking to him for answers. Her gaze darted between everyone in the room.

Clearing his throat and flashing a smile, he said, "Ms. Romano, I am Dr. Kyncade, and this is Dr. Maharaj. You've been in the hospital for a few days."

Staring at him in a combination of disbelief and recognition, she asked, "Why? What happened to me?"

"You, along with four of your staff members, were poisoned," Jai chimed in.

Silence filled the room as they gave her time to process the information. As realization dawned, her angry scowl turned into shock.

Trying to sit up while digesting what she'd heard, Valentina whispered, "Wait a minute, what?"

"Ms. Romano, I'll need you to take your time and not move too fast," Dr. Kyncade said, as he approached the hospital bed. The nurse stepped to the side and allowed room for him. Glancing into her hazel eyes when he was a few inches away, Marcus was as captivated as he'd been when he first saw her at the STEM charity event weeks ago.

Remaining professional and focused on the task at hand, he asked, "How are you feeling?"

"I don't understand." Locking eyes with him, she whispered, "I'm not sure right now. This is a lot to take in."

It took everything in him not to move closer and take her in his arms. She didn't just look scared, Valentina looked lost as if the world had been yanked from under her.

"I understand and know that you may have many questions," he responded. "Let's start there."

After spending about twenty minutes with Valentina, Marcus and Jai checked in on the other patients. They were relieved that everyone was alert and seemed to be doing okay. All of them were looking for an explanation about why they were hospitalized.

Unfortunately, they could not remember what had happened to them. An hour later, Jai and Marcus were back in his office.

"Thank you for consulting on these cases," Marcus said, finally breaking the silence. "I'm glad that I reached out to you."

"You're welcome," Jai replied. "I'm always up for a challenge."

"That's what makes you an exceptional doctor, brother."

"Flattery will get you everywhere, but if you twist my arm, I'm sure I could subject myself to a fantastic dinner at the restaurant we ate in the other night." Jai chuckled and rubbed his stomach. "Seriously, man, I appreciate you giving me the chance to help."

The wall clock ticked as Marcus gathered his thoughts. Clearing his throat, he said, "Can I ask you something on a personal level?"

Smiling, Jai said, "Sure, what is it?"

"I'm curious. Did you ever feel that it was wrong to fall in love with Temple?" he asked.

"No, not at all," Jai responded without hesitation. "Yes, she was a patient at my facility, but her presence in my life is a blessing."

CHAPTER 11

*R*acing through the kitchen, Valentina did a last-minute check on the dishes that her chefs were preparing for tonight's holiday party. Her contributions for this event were her signature desserts that included Italian Cream Cheese, Rum, and Love Cakes.

After her release from the hospital, she dove into work full force. Even though Dr. Kyncade encouraged her to ease back into her daily routine, she didn't listen.

In an hour, she would be on a plane traveling to the States. A few days later, some of her top chefs would join her in Chicago as they prepared for the huge wedding.

Rounding the corner toward the large walk-in pantry without looking up, Valentina ran smack into a wall of hard muscles. Sculpted arms halted her movement. Slowly, her gaze did an ascent from Marcus' chest to his twinkling eyes.

"Is this your idea of easing back into work?" he asked with a raised eyebrow. "I'm sure that I was clear about the instructions I gave you, Ms. Romano."

"Dr. Kyncade, what are you doing here?" she whispered. "I wasn't expecting to see you." *Like, no time soon.*

"Oh, so is that why you're ignoring doctor's orders?" He smirked and arched an eyebrow. "Blatantly, at that."

The usual snazzy comeback escaped Valentina. The handsome man who still held her securely in his arms was a big distraction. Taking a deep breath, she casually stepped out of his embrace.

She smiled. "Things are a little busy and I'm preparing to head out of town, as you know from me sharing that at my last checkup."

Placing a loose strand of hair behind her ear, he said, "Yes, I do. But you still need to take it easy."

Closing her eyes and inhaling the aquatic scent of his cologne, Valentina was immobilized by his soothing and sensual touch. Afraid that the final bit of strength she'd been using to ward off her attraction to the doctor would implode at any time, her mind and body warred with stepping out of his grasp. As she started to rest her cheek against his hand, a deep voice interrupted their intimate moment.

Walking up and inserting himself into the conversation, Lorenzo said in a gruff voice. "Hello, Dr. Kyncade. To what do we owe this visit? Did the hospital run out of patients to see?"

Keeping eye contact with Valentina, he smiled. "No, there are plenty of patients; however, I was only interested in seeing one today."

Sensing the mood change, Valentina shifted her focus to Lorenzo. "Is there something that you need from me right now?"

Surprise flickered in his expression at Valentina's irritated tone. "No, I was checking on you and noticed that we had a visitor."

"Well, as you can see, I'm fine," she said. "My visitor is welcome here." Lorenzo's uncharacteristic behavior baffled Valentina. She was grateful that he took care of things for her personally as well as the business while she'd been out of commission, but the tone he was taking with the good doctor, was out of line.

Lorenzo had confessed his feelings for her in an awkward moment after she was released from the hospital. As much as she loved him as a person, long-time friend, and business partner, she harbored no romantic feelings for him. She was very clear about this with him and sensed that he didn't believe her as much as he should. However, Dr. Kyncade was another story because her feelings for him moved past the friend zone.

Smiling and keeping his cool demeanor, Marcus replied, "It was nice seeing you again, Mr. Ricci. I'm sure it won't be the last time." Then his eyes fell squarely on Valentina.

While letting those words sink in, she didn't miss his intense stare. A bold statement from a confident man. One that she wouldn't mind getting to know better. Right now, Valentina would enjoy these few minutes of banter with him since she'd be out of town for a while.

Lorenzo was still in denial that Valentina had been honest with him about wanting to be friends. Nothing more, nothing less. He poured his heart out to her at the hospital and she had to let him know that those feelings were not reciprocated. She loved him, but not in a romantic manner.

"I've seen how you are doing today, I'll be on my way," Marcus said.

"There's no rush," Valentina replied. "You're welcome to stay a little while longer."

Interjecting himself into the conversation, Lorenzo said, "I believe you have to get ready for a flight, so you don't have that much time to spare."

Turning slightly to face him, she said, "I'm well aware of where I need to be and the amount of time I have to get there. If you can excuse us, I'll check in with you before I leave."

Choosing his battles wisely, Lorenzo nodded at Valentina then glanced at Marcus before walking away from them.

Releasing a low whistle, Marcus said, "Remind me to never make you mad."

"You mean again," she replied with an arched eyebrow. "You didn't forget our brief conservation when we first met, did you?"

Thirty minutes later, she was boarding a private plane at Rome International Airport. It was time to head to Chicago and meet with the bride in person. They'd been video chatting and came to the agreement that Valentina should come into town earlier. As she was settling into her seat, another passenger entered the plane.

Surprise etched across her face. "Dr. Kyncade, what are you doing here?"

"Would you believe me if I told you I was making a house or a plane call?"

She shook her head and looked out the window and a flush of excitement washed over her. Finally she turned and tried to give him her best unbothered look. "No I wouldn't believe you."

"Okay then. Straight talk only. I'm hitching a ride with you to the States," he replied casually. "It appears that you are traveling on one of my good friend's private planes."

"Really, now?" she asked. "Why do I feel this was planned?"

Shrugging, he grinned, then laughed. "As it turns out, I received a special invite to the wedding for helping to save the culinary staff. Especially one beautiful and talented head chef who was handpicked for the joyous occasion."

Seconds later, the cabin door closed, and the pilot announced their departure. Seatbelts fastened, they both got comfortable and shared intense stares, as if trying to penetrate each other's soul.

Once the plane was in the air and at cruising altitude, the flight attendant checked in to see if they needed anything. Valentina asked for a glass of Moscato, while Marcus settled on Cognac. When she was out of earshot, Marcus turned his attention to Valentina. "We have about ten hours flying above the clouds. Let's get to know one another. How do you suggest we fill up all that time?"

After taking a sip of the sweet tasting Moscato, Valentina said,

"Well, Dr. Kyncade, that tone makes the question sound a little suggestive," she teased.

"I want to know everything," he replied. "If I were making any other suggestions, you would know. I wouldn't seduce a woman without making sure that she was fully aware of what she'd be getting into."

Maybe it was the way he said those words or his devilish smile or the scent of his cologne beckoning her closer. Maybe it was none or all of it. Whatever it was, Valentina needed answers and the good doctor sitting little more than a kiss away from her had all of them.

"So, we can start with getting to know one another, then see where that takes us," he continued. "I won't rule out seduction, but it's too early for that."

Crossing her legs, she replied in an enticing manner. "Are you sure you can handle what's in store?"

Leaning forward and keeping his voice low, he said, "Trust me, I can handle that and more when it comes to you."

His tone was everything. It sent a shiver of anticipation up her spine. How could this happen? And so soon? Valentina always tried to be standoffish when it came to men and them wanting a relationship that she didn't have the time for now. Her focus was on growing her business and not having to depend on anyone. She'd also seen what happened when women sacrificed their hope and dreams for a relationship that took more than it gave to them.

Taking a sip of his drink, he said, "Talk to me, Beautiful."

Clearing her throat, she said, "Well, I was born and raised in Rome. My parents owned and operated a chain of successful local restaurants."

"So, cooking came naturally for you?" he asked.

"Yes, it did. Plus my uncle Tomasino Valastro was a world renowned, international baker."

He was enlightened when Valentina shared the history behind something as amazing as wedding cakes—one element that was a major sign of two people becoming one. Wheat and barley cakes were credited with Ancient Rome as their origin. They were broken over the bride's head as a symbol of luck and fertility. Marcus smiled at Valentina's animated expressions and hand gestures as he listened to her with his undivided attention.

"Those are some interesting facts, Valentina," Marcus said after taking a sip of the amber liquid in his glass.

Blushing, she replied, "I'm glad you were enjoying them."

"The company is what I'm enjoying the most." His intense stare caused moisture to pool between her thighs.

Smiling, Valentina replied, "I'm enjoying this time with you as well. Now, it's your turn. Tell me about the enigmatic Dr. Kyncade."

"Trust me, there's nothing mysterious about me. I'm as straightforward as one can be."

Taking a sip of her drink, Valentina studied him for a brief moment. "I find that hard to believe. From what I understand, you have some *hidden* skillsets."

Leaning forward, he grabbed her free hand and replied, "Oh, that I do, and you will find out soon enough."

"Hmm okay. Now, back to my original request. Tell me about yourself."

"Sure, I can do that. My father was a military officer, and I grew up in a number of places. We lived in a number of states as well as overseas."

"That sounds exciting but a little unsettling because of the relocation."

"I didn't really think about it because I was young and that was our lifestyle. We would have a few years in one place then on to the next adventure."

Five hours passed, dinner had been served, and their conversation was still going strong, having covered everything from elementary school to college, professional blunders and victories. It had been a while since she'd enjoyed the company of a man that didn't have a knife or mixing bowl in his hands and was taking direction from her. Finally, Marcus convinced Valentina to go lie down and get some rest in the bedroom.

Rising from her seat, Valentina glanced at Marcus. "I thought your seduction was going to be smoother than that."

"I didn't say that I'd be joining you. Look at your dirty little mind."

"And don't think that I believe your excuse for getting on this plane. You don't know that bride or the groom."

"I don't know what you are talking about."

"Don't play innocent with me."

He stood and smiled. "Innocent. Me? Never."

Glancing over her shoulder as she walked away, she said, "And that's my point."

"Get some rest, Valentina. I'll be right here."

Ninety minutes before landing, the pilot made that announcement and woke them. Valentina showered and changed, then Marcus took his turn in the private bathroom. Spinach, cheese, and mushroom omelets, along with freshly squeezed orange juice and mixed fruit, was their breakfast of choice.

Glancing at Marcus, Valentina said, "I'm glad that you were on this ride with me."

"Oh, beautiful, this ride has just begun," Marcus replied, flashing a smile.

CHAPTER 12

Chef Valentina was putting the finishing touches on tonight's Italian-themed meal. One of the bride's best friends reached out to her because she was hosting a small get-together at a place called the Castle. It was being held in one of the three ballrooms within the structure and decorated in royal blue, gold, and white. Music from different genres was played in the background by one of the top DJs in the nation. He'd also been chosen for the wedding reception.

"Oh my God, this food is delicious," Lola said. "I am so glad that you're here."

"Thank you. I'm glad you're enjoying the meal."

Public relations extraordinaire Lola Samuels had scaled back from her successful entrepreneurial endeavors and focused on her wedding planning. After dealing with the trauma from her kidnapping and eventual rescue, she was looking forward to sharing a happily married life with the man of her dreams. Everyone was worried because Dro and Nasir were still in the Middle East with only days to spare. The last message from the groom was *"Do not cancel the wedding. I will be home on time. Keep the faith."* Lola held onto those words but as the days went on, that faith was wavering a little. Pretty bold move for a bride to continue on with something so huge without a groom in sight.

"I'm looking forward to talking about the cake," she said. "I know it's going to be amazing."

Smiling, Chef Valentina replied. "I can promise you it will be."

After making sure that everyone had enough to eat and enjoyed their meal, she grabbed her coat and stepped onto the second-floor snow dusted balcony. The hired staff could handle things while she took a moment for herself. Closing her eyes and allowing the fresh, frigid air from the nearby snow-covered lake to enter her nostrils, Valentina enjoyed the serenity.

Her thoughts went to Marcus, who had been watching her all night. *"That man."* But he also appeared to be in attendance for something else. Every new person who walked through the door was treated to an eagle-eyed scrutiny that matched the level of a CIA operative. *What was that about?* There was something he was keeping from her. Even Jai was acting the same way. Neither one of them let her out of their sight. And she had tested this theory twice by going into an area that did not warrant their presence.

As if on cue and sensing his presence, Valentina slowly opened her eyes and looked over her shoulder. There he stood, with a contemplative facial expression. Her breath hitched, and she remained silent watching as he walked towards her in a slow, panther-like fashion. She wasn't the only one who followed his movements. Every full-blooded woman within striking distance also had eyes on him.

Standing a few inches apart while looking deep into each other's eyes, their attraction could no longer be denied. She had watched him partake of the Italian Ricotta Meatballs and used slow, methodical movements to taste and savor what she had made. She could only wonder if he was equally precise when it came to making love. Goodness, she needed to get a grip. Marcus and Valentina had been tap-dancing around the inevitable.

Extending his arm after removing his glove, he ran an index finger down her smooth face. "You are so beautiful," he said. His sensually charged tone sent chills throughout her body and heat cascaded down to the core of her pleasure zone.

"Marcus, I don't know what to say," she replied breathlessly.

"Say nothing." Closing the small gap between them, he pulled her into his body and leaned down to plant a luscious kiss on her lips. His tongue entangled with hers as the heat of their kiss escalated into a burning inferno despite the frigid air that surrounded them.

Ending the lip lock, they stood motionless and stared into each other's eyes. No one was quick to speak. After searching her face with his gaze, Marcus asked, "Are you okay?"

"Yes, I'm fine," Valentina answered, placing her hand on his chest, she continued, "This is just surprising for me."

"I hope that was in a good way." He studied her with longing in his eyes.

"It is," she said, smiling as something in her heart opened just a little. Well, maybe more than just a little.

"Since we've established that, I say that we seal this with another kiss," Marcus said and didn't wait for a response. Leaning in, his lips met hers, filled with pure passion. A while later, they came up for air and touched foreheads while trying to slow their breathing.

Valentina glanced up into the mesmerizing brown eyes that were staring into hers. "That was..." Her words abruptly trailed off as a sweet, sensual kiss touched her awaiting lips.

"Otherworldly." He sighed as he pulled her closer. "I can't wait to get you alone and show you how much you mean to me," Marcus shared as his hands traced the curves of her hips.

"Can we leave now? Do you think they will miss us?"

Chuckling and shaking his head, he said, "Yes, I think they would. So, let's make our final rounds and then the rest of the night belongs to us."

"I'm good with that," Valentina said, smiling.

"Come on, let's get back into the warmth of the building," Marcus said while taking in the wintry scenery.

"I feel pretty warm now," she smiled.

Briefly kissing her lips, he replied, "Mm, let's go Temptress." He also noticed movement in his peripheral but kept his composure. As soon as the couple stepped inside the building, Marcus locked eyes with Jai who was in close proximity to them.

Squeezing his hand and sensing that something was wrong, Valentina asked, "What is it?"

"I need you to trust me, okay. Things are about to get a little busy in here."

"Explain ..." Valentina started as the words trailed off when six heavily armed men burst through the doors. Behind them, Lewis Wingate walked in smirking as if he'd won the lottery.

"So, you are having a party without me?" he asked as his gaze landed in their direction.

Visibly shook, she couldn't understand how Marcus and Jai remained calm in the midst of what was happening.

Jai responded. "Actually, you are right on time."

The lights flickered then the unwelcome visitors were disarmed and placed face down on the floor. Each of them surrounded by a King, Knight, or Queen of the Castle who had been wearing the Emperor's Suit device that made them invisible to the naked eye. Wingate stood in shook, realizing that he didn't have the upper hand in this situation. He took off running.

Marcus sprinted, quickly closing the gap between them and wrestled him to the floor. It was like a replay of what happened in Italy.

"This time you won't get away or be able to pay your slim circle of friends to help you."

Laughing, Wingate replied. "I promise you that I will escape again."

"I can guarantee that you won't," Jai said with a penetrating gaze that caused the man to swallow his next words. "You were lucky the first time, not so much now."

Members of the International Joint Crime Task Force entered the room and handcuffed the perpetrators including the two agents that assisted in Wingate's initial escape overseas. After all of the excitement ended and the ballroom was void of the undesirable guests, Lola had the DJ start the music again.

CHAPTER 13

Valentina watched as Marcus and Jai walked through a set of doors, disappearing along with a few of the other Kings and Knights of the Castle. She didn't have a chance to talk to him about what happened. Things had calmed down, but she was still shocked that Lewis Wingate had escaped and been running around free.

"That's why Marcus was on the plane," she whispered.

"Are you okay, Chef Valentina?" Lola asked.

"Yes, I'm fine. Glad that things have calmed down."

"Me too, but we knew that they were coming."

Surprise crossing her face, Valentina began, "How is ....?

Holding up her hand, Lola said, "I can't talk about it. But nobody gets close to the Castle unless they are allowed in."

Many questions floated through Valentina's mind. However, she understood that there were rules about information that couldn't be shared with her. Frustrating as it was, the bottom line is everyone was safe. Being a witness to the heroic actions of the Castle and Marcus' involvement elevated her interest in getting closer to him.

Deciding to change the conversation, Valentina asked Lola, "Has everything been to your liking this evening? Is there anything else that you'd like me to take care of?"

"No, we are good. You have done an amazing job."

She smiled. "Thank you, I love to hear that."

"Relax and enjoy the rest of the party," Lola said. "Besides, I think that there is a handsome doctor waiting to spend some time with you."

Blushing, she slowly turned as Lola quietly slipped away. Valentina met the intense stare of Marcus. He stalked over to her like a panther ready to devour its prey.

"May I have this dance?" he asked.

"Yes," she answered in a breathless manner.

They danced, talked, and she was introduced to more of the Kings, Knights, and Queens of the Castle. Everything that happened earlier was forgotten or at least pushed to the back burner. No more thoughts about Wingate or interruptions to the evening. Tomorrow was a new day. Tonight, she'd focus on becoming one with the man who captured her attention and penetrated her heart.

As the party wound down, Marcus and Valentina said their goodbyes and headed to the house that he was renting for the duration of their stay in Chicago. She didn't object, even though she'd been staying in a downtown luxury hotel. They decided to take the next step and quench the desire flowing between them.

* * *

ACROSS THE ROOM, Lorenzo had been watching the couple all night. He arrived in the States early yesterday to assist with the final culinary preparations for the party. Valentina's conversation with him was strictly professional. There was a strain on their relationship since he declared his love for her and she had to tell him she didn't return his feelings. Witnessing all that had transpired tonight and the way that Marcus protected her, Lorenzo realized that their feelings were much deeper, even in such a short amount of time. He would figure out how to move forward without causing any more friction in their friendship and business partnership.

Turning to walk in the direction of the kitchen, he came face to face with a gorgeous brunette woman with legs that seemed to go on forever and eyes the color of a clear sky.

Smiling, she gave him an appraising once over before she locked gazes with him and asked, "Can I buy you a drink?"

Amused by the twinkle of mischief in her eyes, he responded, "It's an open bar."

"That's right, that means the drinks are on them, but the conversation is on me."

Lorenzo roared with laughter. Once she looped her arm through his, they made their way to the bar.

CHAPTER 14

Fire and Ice lived in his kiss. Hands caressed her body, causing her to squirm in delight. His masterful hands slowly traced her curves, and his lips left a sensuous trail of desire that she knew he would quench. Grabbing a handful of the sheets, Valentina moaned as Marcus brought her to the brink of ecstasy with his skillful tongue.

"Does that feel good?" he asked. "Do you want me to stop?"

"Yes, no" she whispered.

Stopping his movements right above her belly button, Marcus chuckled, "Baby, which is it? Yes, or no?"

Before she could answer, his tongue began a pleasurable trail down to the center of her core. Her hips tried to rise off the bed, but Marcus's muscular arms held them in place. He feasted as if this was his last meal.

Minutes later, he entered her, and they spent the rest of the night enjoying each other. Making love until they were exhausted. Waking up the next morning, they took an extended shower and ate breakfast together. Feeling energized, Valentina fixed them

French toast, scrambled eggs, fresh fruit, and freshly squeezed orange juice.

"Um, this is good, baby," he said.

Valentina smiled. "I'm glad that you are enjoying the food."

"You know I enjoy all kinds of nourishment," Marcus replied seductively. "Didn't I prove that last night and this morning?"

Arching her left eyebrow, she said, "You did all right."

After swallowing his food, Marcus placed his fork on the white ceramic plate. "Really? Do I need to give you a quick reminder of my skills?"

"As tempting as that is, we have plans," she said. "The sooner we get going, then we can get back and indulge in some more fun."

"You know we can skip those plans and just stick to the indoor fun all day," he said glancing at Valentina. "You know it's cold outside and more snow is expected today so we could stay in keep each other warm."

"Why are you trying to change my mind?" she asked, watching him approach her.

"Because after last night and this morning, I don't want to share you with anyone," Marcus said, looking deeply into her eyes. "At least not today. Jai and Temple would understand."

Running her hand slowly down his face and chest, she said, "I would really like to get to know them better. Besides, aren't I worth the wait?"

"Hmm, you are definitely that and much more," he replied sweetly, kissing her lips. "Do you need help with the dishes?"

"No, I got this. Let your friends know we will see them shortly."

"I will. Just know that you will owe me."

Winking and blowing him a kiss as he backed out of the kitchen, "I plan to pay up with interest, Dr. Kyncade."

Over the past few weeks, her life faced several twists and turns. Never expecting to find the man of her dreams, she'd always focused on business. Now, in a short span of time, she found love with Marcus. Her saving grace, protector, and soulmate.

OPERATION LOTUS

Chapter 1

"Unbelievable! Dro is moving around so much it's almost impossible to nail down a rescue plan."

Noelle Jakob glanced at her cousin as she delivered the bad news. Everything had been crazy since Dro and the father of Lola's friend hadn't made it out of Ajid—a country in the Middle East.

"He's changing locations regularly to avoid getting caught by the government and possibly killed." Mia Atwood pushed back from the desk, stretched, then continued typing.

Noelle swept her long braids over one shoulder, shot to her feet and grabbed a printout before moving toward Mia. They were in one of three temporary command centers set up in a Bella Russe Hotel's penthouse suite. "Then I should be making sure the team has whatever they need to rescue them and so they make it in time for the wedding."

She stared at Mia and tossed the picture of lotus flowers and the email printout on the laptop keys. "Not searching for these."

Noelle couldn't believe they pulled her off logistics for something as simple as this.

"If you don't want to be a part of Operation Lotus, then just say so." Mia stood, glaring her displeasure. "Because there are two parts to this mission. One." She lifted an index finger. "Getting the groom and company state side for the big event." Mia raised another finger. "Two. Getting those flowers to the reception venue."

"My skills could be put to better use on the recovery team than procuring flowers." She crossed both arms over her chest, hoping her cousin would put a word in with the boss, Daron Kincaid, to return her to the original assignment.

Noelle had become close to Dro in the year she worked at Crossroads Security and met him through events at the Castle, which was a global organization with a humanitarian mission. He'd been teaching her Spanish, and now her vocabulary went beyond *hola* and *adiós*. Dro had been helping to track down her father's side of the family, which she believed were from San Miguel de Allende, the same city in Mexico the Reyes' family were from. She felt driven to do all she could to bring him home.

"Daron entrusted the assignment to me, and I gave it to you." Mia snatched the papers from the keyboard. "Did I select the wrong person?"

"No." Noelle took the documents and headed to her station, resigned to fully commit to the new project. "Please, keep me in the loop."

"This florist is the one Calvin hired for our wedding." Mia's dark-brown eyes softened as she spoke about her husband and reclaimed her chair. "From everything I heard via Lola's wedding coordinator, Kathy, Violet's on top of things. For her to drop off the map and then none of her clients have seen or heard from her in days, something else is going on."

Noelle suddenly felt bad for being so focused on Dro that she forgot he might not be the only one who needed a miracle for the holidays. "I'm on it."

She understood the importance of finding the florist, but Noelle's primary focus was the flowers. If locating the lotuses took some of the pressure off her partner so he could conduct the search, then she'd play her part. It wouldn't stop her hunting for a loophole to get back to the original duties. Noelle was hoping if she could find the lotus flowers for the reception, then maybe she could convince Mia to leave her partner to find the florist on his own.

"The quicker you take care of this, the faster you'll be back on the logistics team." Mia's focus went back on the screen.

Noelle tried to take Mia at her word but wondered if her cousin couldn't see past the girl who was always in trouble and making the wrong choices, to the woman she'd actually become. Uncle Mason had convinced Mia to give her this chance, and she was determined to make her family proud for once. No one but her uncle knew she used to run illegal merchandise for her ex-boyfriend, Rafael, through a global network and almost landed in prison. Noelle was glad her uncle set her straight and kept it out of the family rumor mill.

She shook off the past and tackled the list of flower shops first. After seven failed attempts to locate what they wanted, she scoured the internet. When the online floral results were a casket arrangement and a bouquet with orchids, not lotuses, she realized tracking down the florist may be the quickest solution to getting back on logistics where the real action happened. She shot off a message via the company chat app to Zane Hargrave, the man she'd partnered up with for this task, to see if he'd found anything. He replied saying he was following a lead.

Noelle noticed the report didn't say if someone else was working in the floral shop. Or whether it was open. She dialed the number on file.

"Hello this is Harris at A Sacred Heart Flower and Gifts. How may I help you?"

"What are your hours of operation?" When he replied, she jotted down his name and information on a sticky note and said, "Thank you."

Noelle slipped the phone into her pocket, then grabbed her coat, purse, and boots from under the desk. "I'm going to talk to the floral assistant to see if I can get better answers face to face."

Mia glanced over her shoulder. "I'll be going to The Castle to help Calvin with some amendments to certain gear we'll need to get Dro home."

"Tell your hubby, I said hola." She scanned the desk to make sure she hadn't left anything she'd need, then peeked out of the master bedroom. The hallway was empty, so she dashed into the entertainment room down the hall, past the other bedroom where another workstation was setup until she made it into the living room's foyer.

"Jingle Bells."

That name was the first sign she hadn't made a clean escape.

"You're not leaving without me, are you?" The six-foot muscular man with captivating dark-brown eyes jogged towards the door.

"Sí. Heading to Sacred Heart Flower shop."

"Holly." He glanced down at her and scowled. "You're not a team player."

The man called her everything but her name. She had become tired of trying to correct him. Noelle tried her best not to roll her eyes as she slipped off her indoor shoes and put on a pair of boots and winter gear. "Zane, you're responsible for tracking down Violet."

"As a team *we're* ..." He waved a hand between the two of them. "... supposed to work together to handle both."

Noelle frowned. Zane was sexy as hell for a man with shoulder length hair, which wasn't her thing, but he annoyed the mess out of her. "I thought you were researching something."

"I was, which is why I came to find you." He grabbed a winter vest off the coat rack.

Noelle opened the door, heading to the elevator. Without glancing over her shoulder, she could feel him following her.

"I asked myself ..." He stuck an arm in the open elevator, allowing her to enter first before stepping in and using his keycard to press the parking level reserved for Crossroads Security. "... Could there be a legit reason besides a lost phone that would cause our florist not to pick up when her people called?"

"And what answer did you come up with, Einstein?" She took in his strong jawline, hating and loving how her senses always came to life any time he was near. The sensual, spicy scent coming off him tickled her nose. Noelle hadn't been attracted to an Asian man before, but like a heat-seeking missile Zane drew her in from the first moment she saw him. Whenever he was in a room she couldn't stop checking him out, which was why she tried to avoid him. The last thing she needed was a work relationship to go wrong and lose the ground she gained with her family, and in her career.

He retrieved a set of keys from a vest pocket. "I checked to see if there were any cell tower outages with her provider near the flower shop or her apartment building, but there were none."

Noelle made a mental note to check the morgues on the way to the flower shop. No one wanted to go there yet. She hoped she wouldn't have to deliver any bad news.

Zane gently guided her away from her Hyundai Elantra to the company issued Lexus NX.

"Excuse me. You're the ride along. Not me." Noelle turned, heading toward the Elantra.

He chuckled. "If you wanted to be the driver, then you should have signed out a company vehicle."

"We're only going to a flower shop." Noelle put a hand on one hip preparing to stand her ground.

"A woman has gone missing." Zane tilted his head and frowned as though she'd lost her mind. "This is not a normal flower run, Holly."

Noelle huffed as he nodded to the passenger side of the Lexus. "Fine. I hope you're better at following GPS than you are at remembering names."

Download the last book in the Promise Me a Miracle Series:
https://books2read.com/Operationlotus

PROMISE ME A MIRACLE SERIES

Jaxon Malone lands the simplest job of his career—travel to the Kingdom of Ajid and escort Alia Fadel back to America to be the maid of honor in their friends' wedding. But no one foresaw a previous regime suddenly surging back to power over the country—or their decision to imprison Alia for standing up to the new rulers. Silenced and alone, Alia loses hope of ever being free again.

Jax springs into action, but every attempt to get Alia out of the country fails. Things go from bad to worse when Ajid's Supreme Leader insists on marrying her in a ruthless power play of a publicly televised ceremony.

Jax needs help—and fast. Several Kings of the Castle rise to the call, traveling behind enemy lines to rescue Alia and her family. But it'll take a miracle to pull off their daring escape plan, which must happen before the new government seals the country off from the rest of the world. Is it too late, even for the Kings, to enact the impossible?

https://books2read.com/operationbutterfly

Someone is trying to kill Dr. Sydney Lomax. The award-winning jeweler and inventor accepts a special assignment from Dro Reyes: transport his custom-made wedding rings across a lake of fire. But neither is aware that the job involves mortal danger. Sydney's enemies are determined to succeed, since her mission across the sands of Durabia threatens their secret munitions dump—where a Doomsday Bomb is silently ticking.

Ethan Wakefield, tasked with finding the government's covert facility that's filled with Sydney's inventions, is assigned to protect yet use her. He must locate her tech, which could save or destroy countless lives, before time runs out. But lines get quickly blurred, and now Ethan and Sydney's newfound love is also at risk of destruction in a deadly game of cat and mouse.

As time winds down, Ethan does everything in his power to bring Sydney home alive—but this time, even his best effort might not be good enough.

https://books2read.com/Operationdiamond

PROMISE ME A MIRACLE SERIES

OPERATION IVORY
J.L. CAMPBELL

Michele DaCosta, bridal gown designer extraordinaire receives the commission of her life—except that it's impossibly last-minute. On top of a stressed bride dealing with ghosts from her past, there's also a high-level blizzard attacking all of Chicago, trapping Michele with an over-protective bodyguard.

Rajay Chamani's assignment is to shield the pretty fashion designer from the stalker who ruined a family heirloom and is now determined to use Michele as a messenger to the bride. The situation intensifies when the groom goes missing in action in the Middle East, and Rajay and Michele end up being snowed in. He's blindsided by one more complication: his growing attraction to Michele, simmering hotter even as Mother Nature has the last icy laugh.

Only weeks remain before Chicago's biggest society wedding of the year. Can Rajay and Michele work together to defeat a stalker, defy a blizzard, and finish the world's most elaborate bridal gown to ensure wedding bells win over doomsday knells?

https://books2read.com/Operationivory

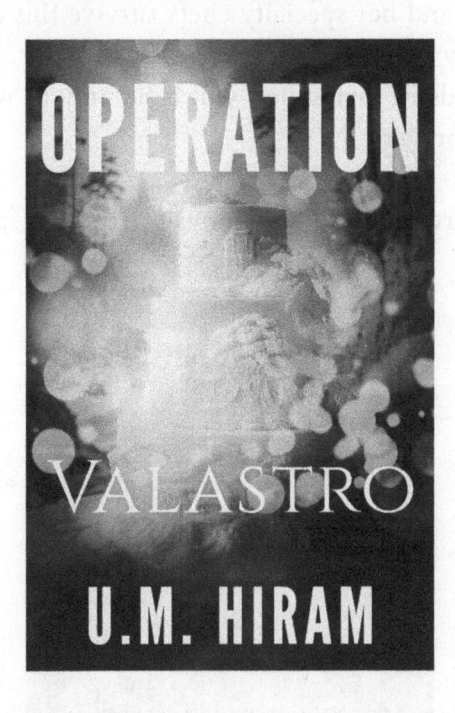

Valentina Romano, a world-famous celebrity chef, is hired to prepare the meal and signature cake for the wedding of Dro Reyes and his fiancée, Lola Samuels. But days before the celebration, she and her four specialty chefs are flat on their backs in an Italian hospital after falling eerily ill.

Dr. Marcus Kyncade, known for his advances in neurotoxins, is the attending physician for the five new patients. His attraction to Valentina is undeniable, but he's shut down by the woman's long-time business associate—and time's relentless scythe.

But to save Valentina's life, he has to beat the blade. He must win a frantic race against the clock to not only find an antidote to a mysterious poison, but also determine exactly who wants Valentina dead.

Will Valentina and her specialty chefs survive this attack from an invisible enemy in time to prepare a feast fit for a King? And if Marcus succeeds in saving her, will it be only to watch her walk out of his life forever?

https://books2read.com/Operationvalastro

OPERATION LOTUS
KAREN D. BRADLEY

Noelle Jakob is livid when she's abruptly pulled from a high-profile assignment to locate a vanished VIP bridegroom. The logistics genius for Crossroads Security, tasked with finding the event's missing florist instead, isn't any happier about having to partner with Zane Hargrave. The one man who makes it impossible for her to focus is now her key to solving this mystery and getting back to her original mission.

Easier said than done.

The closer Noelle and Zane's leads get them to their target, the deeper the danger they encounter. With the florist in trouble and the high-profile wedding fast approaching, it's going to take a holiday miracle to align the stars and ensure the event is a "full-blooming" success.

https://books2read.com/Operationlotus

KINGS OF THE CASTLE

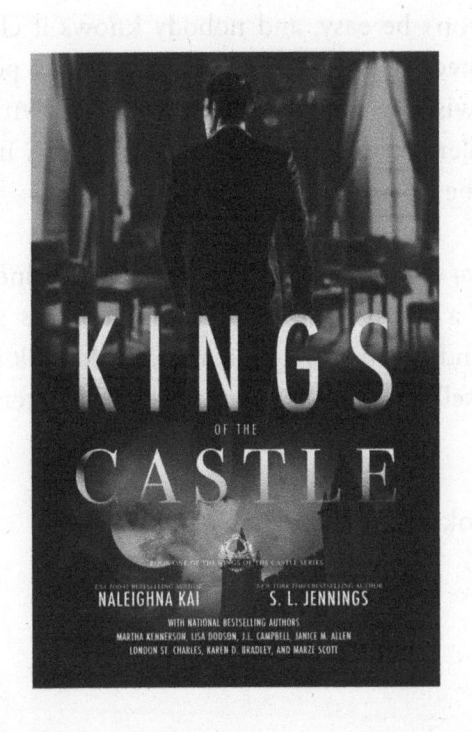

The Castle: elite, elusive ... dangerous.

A secret organization which once stood for protection and benevolence, The Castle has now been corrupted by crime, greed, and dirty politics. Every crime syndicate and dirty politician on earth are determined to control the massive fortune guarded by The Kings: a found family forged by fate but called to action by crisis.

When their mentor ends up on the business end of an assassination attempt, nine men are summoned to right old wrongs and track those responsible. The Kings of the Castle, now grown into captains of industry and leaders of men across Chicago, bring their unique skill sets to the daring mission to bring their enemies down—even if they have to rack up a body count to do it.

The job won't be easy, and nobody knows it clearer than the women destined to love each of these men. As powerful forces conspire to twist the Castle's riches for their own good, convictions are challenged and relationships are tested. In the end, will the sacrifices be worth it?

The Kings of the Castle is a series of self-contained stories with characters in a shared world full of high-stakes suspense, fast-paced plots, and breathtaking romance. Each book is written by a national bestselling author and features a different King of the Castle.

https://books2read.com/Kingsofthecastle

Mariano "Reno" DeLuca uses his skills and resources to create safe havens for women in dangerous situations—until a surge in Chatham's criminal activity threatens the safety and anonymity for the residents of The Second Chance at Life Women's Shelter. Though Reno finally admits that the shelter must be relocated, the crisis couldn't be more ill-timed. Just when he's summoned back to The Castle to meet with his brothers in the secret society, a new woman lands on the shelter's doorstep. Immediately drawn to the mysterious beauty, he struggles to refocus on The Castle's newest challenge: an immoral takeover attempt by an enemy who's supposed to be an ally.

Zuri Okusanya, a Tanzanian Princess, has snuck into America with nothing but the clothes on her back and handwritten instructions from her deceased mother. Desperate for refuge from an arranged marriage by her politically motivated father, the princess has survived a near-death experience to land at the door of the

Chatham shelter, unwilling to trust anyone except Mariano DeLuca.

Reno is conflicted. His fugitive princess is as beautiful as she is intelligent, and her plight speaks straight to his soul—not a vulnerability he can afford with so many lives now at stake. Though he strives not to lose his heart to the forbidden goddess, destiny has other plans.

Will Mariano have the fortitude to defeat his adversaries and save the women of the shelter—now including the woman he loves—or will time win and strip him of everything and everyone he holds dear?

https://books2read.com/kingofchatham

Shaz Bostwick prides himself on his moral compass and business ethics—but both are deeply challenged from the moment Camilla Gibson walks into his office, urgently seeking his help.

Camila has no choice but to throw herself on Shaz's mercy. Though she's a renowned blogger for her world adventures and colorful modeling gigs, this is one instance that fame won't solve. Her daughter, Ayanna, needs specialized treatment in Chicago, but time—and the authorities-- aren't on her side. She's elated when the charming but tough lawyer pledges his support.

Shaz, raised as an immigrant, knows the heartache of family separation firsthand. He's moved by Camila's plight, and calls in favors as the clock ticks down. In return, he's presented with a disturbing offer: let baby Ayanna slip through the cracks in exchange for a handsome reward. The call gives him a tip about an illegal adoption ring, but he can only bust the criminals with the help of his brothers from The Castle.

Fed up with politicians and businessmen with too much money and too little scruples, Shaz mobilizes his friends with astounding speed. His tenacity and intelligence move Camila to her core, igniting an attraction she never thought she'd know again—but there's no way she can act on the sparks with the threat deportation still looming for Ayanna and her.

Shaz Bostwick has a fierce reputation for making a way when there is none—but will his legislative superpower be enough to forge a future with his adventurous Camila?
https://books2read.com/KingofEvanston

Doctor Jaidev Maharaj's life takes a dark turn when a coma patient becomes pregnant, propelling him into media infamy. His troubles are tripled when law enforcement and the government join the clamor—and that's before he learns about the attempt on his mentor's life. When he resolves to chase the details, Jai is thrust into a secret brotherhood that belongs to a world he never conceived—and a destiny that suddenly demands more than he's prepared to give.

Temple Devaughn awakens from a year-long coma to discover she has a child—whom she doesn't remember conceiving. The police suspect foul play at the medical center where she was cared for, but to find the truth Temple must trust Jai Maharaj: a stranger who may or may not have her best interests at heart.

As a dark family secret threatens to sabotage Jai and Temple's quest for the truth, they are pulled toward each other in ways they cannot deny—but betrayals, setbacks, and endless mysteries mar every attempt they make to connect. When unseen enemies conspire to silence Temple for good, true values are tested. Will Jai prove to Temple—and himself—that their love is worth fighting for?

ABOUT THE KINGS OF THE CASTLE SERIES:

Each book from 2-9 is a standalone story in the same world, with no cliffhangers.

https://books2read.com/KingofDevon

Two things threaten to destroy most of Daron Kincaid's life: the tracking device he developed to locate human trafficking victims, and an inherited membership in a mysterious outfit called The Castle.

The new developments come with awful timing. After years with Interpol and the FBI, including a sizable sting that brought down notorious criminals, Daron's ready to move on and build a new life with the love of his life, Cameron Stone. But even after years of security expertise, he's not prepared for Marquise Sinclair's treachery. The international crime boss is determined to take Daron's position in the Castle by leveraging Cameron's life against a project worth billions.

Yet even the savvy Sinclair is utterly unaware about Cameron's unique talents: her loveliness conceals highly specialized training to make men weak or put them on the wrong side of the grave. She's not the only one with secrets. When Daron hides key details from Cameron and his inner circle, the deception only complicates an already tumultuous situation.

Can Daron take on Marquise, manage his loyalty to the Castle, and keep deep confidences without permanently losing the woman he loves?

https://books2read.com/Kingofmorganpark

Real estate developer Kaleb Valentine is known for working lifestyle magic, turning failing communities into thriving havens in the Metro Detroit area. He's on track to become one of the city's most renowned success stories—until a suspicious house fire in one of his properties leaves nothing but charred wreckage and five bodies.

Suddenly in the center of an intense criminal investigation, Kaleb is forced to revisit the harsh life he barely escaped as a teen. Life gets even more complicated when he volunteers at the The Second Chance at Life Women's Shelter—and meets a woman who fascinates him like no other.

Skyler Pierson has no time for romance, let alone love—so nobody's more surprised than she when Kaleb Valentine shows up and instantly puts his charm to work on the walls around her heart. But when the dashing entrepreneur asks her for a favor, she's curious and asks questions—too many of them. The danger she'd thought long-gone from her world is back with a vengeance, worsened by mysterious influences from Kaleb's dark past, as well.

Everything is on the line. How far will Kaleb's enemies go to take him—and his new love—down for good?

https://books2read.com/u/4DDl9g

Grant Khambrel, a sexy, successful Texas architect, has worked hard to build a thriving business, only to learn that dirty strings were attached to his seed money—ties it's taken him years to severe.

When the firm wins the prestigious multi-million-dollar

contract to renovate the city's United Center, it should be a reason for celebration, but the past Grant never asked for becomes the inescapable firestorm of his present. Rumors of improper business ethics cast shadows on his company's reputation, intensified when Grant is blackmailed by a powerful local politician.

None of it's the best foot to start out on when meeting the most gorgeous woman he's ever seen.

Autumn Knight, the savvy and beautiful Administrative Director of the United Center, grew up around both sides of Chicago politics. Though her father, a powerful real estate tycoon and alderman, continues to pressure her for under-the-table kickbacks, Autumn is steadfast about her ethics—though that manifesto is harder to maintain when she meets charismatic Grant Khambrel.

The intense man, preselected by her father's committee for the Center's new project, is everything she craves and nothing she can want. Though their chemistry is overwhelming from the start, she doesn't dare trust her heart to a person with such an uncertain past. When more lies and secrets surface, exploring even a casual romance with the gorgeous architect is out of the question.

Will Grant prove to Autumn that he's hero she desires and deserves—or will his tainted success be the ruination of the future they long to believe in?

https://books2read.com/Kingoflincolnpark2

Alejandro "Dro" Reyes has been a "fixer" for as long as he can remember, which makes him perfectly suited to own a crisis management company focused on repairing professional reputations. Business in the Windy City is booming—until a mysterious call following an attempt on his mentor's life forces him to drop everything and accept a position with The Castle. Though his family has been affiliated with the secret organization for decades, his new involvement leads to being blindsided by an enemy he never saw coming.

Lola Samuels, the polished public relations maven of Chicago's elite, sets aside her growing attraction to Dro in the name of seeking assistance for her newest assignment. Longtime bad boy Shawn Mayhew needs some fast shine on his tarnished image: a simple enough job if she and Dro tag-team the essentials, right?

But sometimes, success really is in the details.

Lola is totally unaware of the animosity between the Mayhews and the Reyes —until it's too late. The cut-and-dry job is quickly spun into a sticky web of danger and deceptions—most prominently, Dro's scheme to use their working relationship to gain intel on his enemy.

When Lola discovers she's a pawn in Shawn and Dro's dangerous game, she's conflicted—yet then captured. Alejandro's carefully controlled world is thrown into chaos, and he vows to use every resource in his arsenal, including the skills of the eight men with whom he's just reconnected, to rescue the woman he desperately loves.

https://books2read.com/u/bQe9W7

Dwayne Harper's passion is giving disadvantaged boys the tools to transform themselves into successful men. But when he steps up to take his place among The Kings of the Castle—the men he considers brothers—politics and personalities clash, conspiring against him.

Tiffany Mason is also harboring a dark secret that can shatter Dwayne's ultimate dream, not to mention the depths of his heart. While Dwayne is everything she could want in a handsome, intelligent, and driven man, details from her past have her doubting her worthiness of his marriage proposal. Complicating matters are new accusations against Dwayne, testing his dedication to his cause.

Enter a female acquaintance who's determined to help Dwayne persevere, but her methods become questionable when she uses blackmail to achieve her goals—leveraging Tiffany's scandalous past in her jealousy-driven war chest. Exposed to Dwayne in this insidious manner, Tiffany has no right to recourse, and can only hope Dwayne chooses her as his queen for life.

One woman holds the key to his success; the other will guide him to the cliff of his downfall. It will be the full test of Dwayne Harper's character to discern the difference—and claim his due success as a King of The Castle.

https://books2read.com/King-of-Lawndale

ABOUT THE KINGS OF THE CASTLE SERIES:
Each book from 2-9 is a standalone story in the same world, with no cliffhangers.
https://geni.us/Kingsofthecastleseries

KNIGHTS OF THE CASTLE

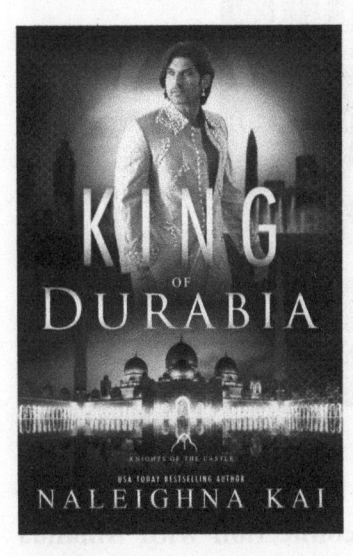

No good deed goes unpunished, or that's how Ellena Kiley feels after she rescues a child and the former Crown Prince of Durabia offers to marry her. He is given nine days in order to make her fall in love with him.

Kamran learns of a nefarious plot to undermine his position with the Sheikh and jeopardize his ascent to the throne. He's unsure how Ellena, the fiery American seductress, fits into the plan but she's a secret weapon he's unwilling to relinquish.

Ellena connection to Kamran challenges her ideals, her freedoms, and her heart. Plus, loving him makes her a potential target for his enemies. When Ellena is kidnapped, Kamran is forced to bring in the Kings.

In the race against time to rescue his woman and defeat his enemies, the kingdom of Durabia will never be the same.

Visit https://books2read.com/Kingofdurabia
  to download your copy.

Chaz Maharaj is caught between keeping his public image intact and his heart's desires. The connection with Amanda should have ended with that unconditional "hall pass" which led to one night of unbridled passion. When Amanda walked out of his life, it was supposed to be forever. Neither of them could have anticipated fate's plan.

As Chaz tries to pursue a relationship with her, he's faced with obstacles from his ex-wife and a vicious plot that threatens both their love and Amanda's life. With the help of the Kings of the Castle, Chaz must navigate the treacherous waters of love and deception to protect his newfound love and find a way to be together forever.

Will their love be strong enough to withstand the challenges ahead, or will they be torn apart by forces beyond their control?

https://books2read.com/Knightofbronzeville

When the Kings of the Castle recommend Calvin Atwood, strategic defense inventor, to create a security shield for the kingdom of Durabia, it's the opportunity of a lifetime. The only problem—it's a two-year assignment and he promised his fiancée they would step away from their dangerous lifestyle and start a family.

Security specialist, Mia Jakob, adores Calvin with all her heart, but his last assignment put both of their lives at risk. She understands how important this new role is to the man she loves, but the thought that he may be avoiding commitment does cross her mind.

Calvin was sure he'd made the best decision for his and Mia's future, until enemies of the state target his invention and his woman. Set on a collision course with hidden foes, this Knight will need the help of the Kings to save both his Queen and the Kingdom of Durabia.

https://books2read.com/KnightofSouthHolland

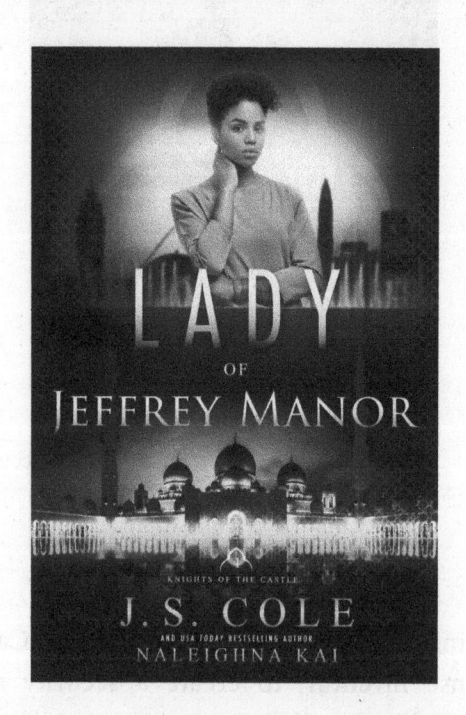

Blair Swanson never expected to find love while on a temporary assignment in the Kingdom of Durabia. But when she meets Hassan, the kingdom's most eligible bachelor, sparks fly between them. Despite his duty to marry for political reasons, Hassan finds himself drawn to the practical and courageous American nurse.

As their feelings for each other deepen, a dark secret threatens to tear them apart. Hassan is torn between his duty to the throne and his love for Blair. With their future hanging in the balance, Blair and Hassan must navigate the complexities of love and duty in a world where nothing is as it seems. Can he find a way to save the woman he loves and fulfill his royal obligations?

Join Blair and Hassan on their journey of love, sacrifice, and discovering what truly matters in Lady of Jeffrey Manor, a heart-warming romance novel that will leave you swooning.

https://books2read.com/Ladyofjefferymanor

Someone is killing women and the villain's next target strikes too close to the Kingdom of Durabia.

Dorian "Ryan" Bostwick is a protector and he's one of the best in the business. When a King of the Castle assigns him to find his former lover, Aziza, he stumbles upon a deadly underworld operating close to the Durabian border.

Aziza Hampton had just rekindled her love affair with Ryan when a night out with friends ends in her kidnapping. Alone and scared, she must find a way to escape her captor and reunite with her lover.

In a race against time, Ryan and the Kings of the Castle follow ominous clues into the underbelly of a system designed to take advantage of the vulnerable. Failure isn't an option and Ryan will rain down hell on earth to save the woman of his heart.

http://books2read.com/KOPI

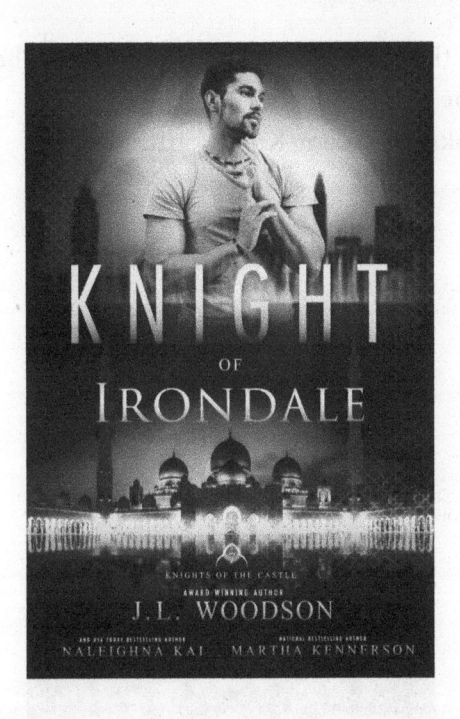

Neesha Carpenter is running from her stalker ex-boyfriend, but now the police have named her the prime suspect in his shooting. With her life in danger and everything spinning out of control, she runs into her high school sweetheart, Christian Vidal, and turns to him for help.

Christian has always been drawn to Neesha's strength, intelligence, and beauty, and he offers her safe haven in the kingdom of Durabia, protecting her from both the danger of her ex and the accusations against her. He enlists the help of the Kings of the Castle to keep her safe, but as their rekindled romance heats up, mounting evidence points to Neesha's guilt. Meanwhile, Neesha's stay in the country puts the royal family at odds with the American government.

As Christian tries to uncover the truth and clear Neesha's name, he must confront the hard question: did the woman he loves pull the trigger, or is she being framed?

https://books2read.com/Knightofirondale

Rahm Fosten is finally free after serving time for a crime he didn't commit. His priority is taking care of the women who supported him during his hellish journey, and pursuing a relationship with Marilyn Spears. But as he tries to settle into his dream life as a Knight of the Castle, old enemies are waiting in the shadows. An unexpected twist threatens to tear Rahm and Marilyn apart just as they are finally together.

Meanwhile, Rahm's Aunt Alyssa travels to Durabia and catches the eye of Ahmad Maharaj, a wealthy surgeon who is on the cutting edge of the medical industry. But attending a private Bliss event puts her in danger and under the watchful eye of a deadly enemy.

As Rahm and Marilyn navigate their romance, they must also protect their loved ones from a vengeful adversary. The Kings of the Castle are on high alert, ready to do whatever it takes to keep Marilyn, Alyssa, and Rahm's family safe.

Join Rahm and Marilyn on their journey of love and danger in Knight of Grand Crossing, and Alyssa and Ahmad in this heart-pounding international suspense novel

https://books2read.com/Knightofgrandcrossing

Single mothers who are eligible for release, have totally disappeared from the Alabama justice system. Women's advocate, Meghan Turner, has uncovered a disturbing pattern and she's desperate for help. Then her worse nightmare becomes a horrific reality when her friend goes missing under the same mysterious circumstances.

Rory Tannous has spent his life helping society's most vulnerable. When he learns of Meghan's dilemma, he takes it personal. Rory has his own tragic past and he'll utilize every connection, even the King of the Castle, to help this intriguing woman find her friend and the other women.

As Rory and Meghan work together, the attraction grows and so does the danger. The stakes are high and they will have to risk their love and lives to defeat a powerful adversary.

https://books2read.com/Knightofbirmingham2

Following an undercover FBI sting operation that didn't go as planned, Agent Mateo Lopez is ready to put the government agency in his rearview mirror.

A confirmed workaholic, his career soared at the cost of his love life which had crashed and burned until mutual friends arranged a date with beautiful, sharp-witted, Rachel Jordan, a rising star at a children's social services agency.

Unlucky in love, Rachel has sworn off romantic relationships, but Mateo finds himself falling for her in more ways than one. When trouble brews in one of Rachel's cases, he does everything in his power to keep her safe—even if it means resorting to extreme measures.

Will the choices they make bring them closer together or cost them their lives?

https://books2read.com/Knight-of-Penn-Quarter

QUEENS OF THE CASTLE

ABOUT THE QUEENS OF THE CASTLE SERIES

Each Queen book is a standalone, without cliffhangers

USA TODAY, **and National Bestselling Authors have created a world where women can—and will have it all—love, family, career, and leave a legacy while overcoming generational challenges.**

Someone is sabotaging Dr. Lani Jamison's career and their tactics are escalating. Are the attacks attempts to prevent Lani from working with The Castle to implement robotic surgery in the hospital? Or does her association with Jordan Spears have his clients seeking to take her out of the picture?

Jordan lives a complicated life from his family dynamics to his "interesting" career. When Lani tries to distance herself from him, he's forced to temporarily accept it as he staves off the hostile demands of his brother who has racked up debt with the criminals who won't take no for an answer. Will Jordan be able to convince Lani that their relationship deserves a chance despite its origins? And will Lani survive an unknown enemy's endeavor to put her six feet under?

https://books2read.com/QueenofLahaina

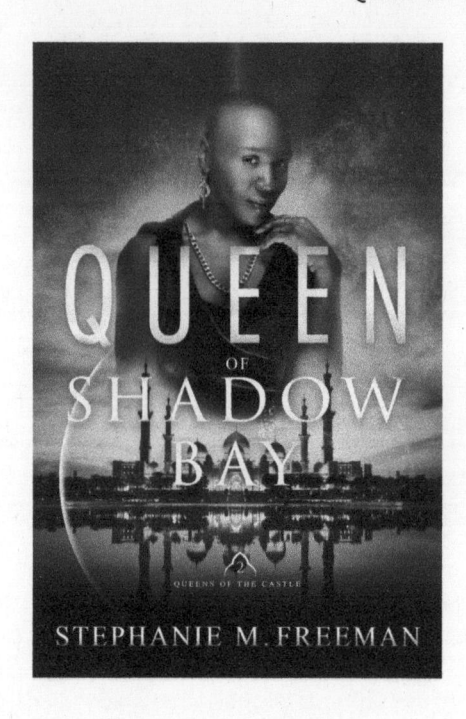

Not all monsters are born, some are made.

Killing Carpathia was the first mistake. Informing her niece made it worse. Durabia meant a fresh start for Raye Bennett. One phone call destroyed all of that. Returning to American soil could send her back to prison for the rest of her life. Attending the funeral of a family member may be deadlier. Heaven and Hell change places in this romantic thriller where the poison is sweeter than the wine.

https://books2read.com/QueenofShadowBay

Solange Porter never believed her husband, Emeril would betray her. But he did. First, he died when he promised they'd be together forever. Then, he left her as the head of a tech company that she didn't want to lead. She wasn't alone; most of the staff felt the same way.

Computer programmer Wale Adisa needs Solange's help. To get it, he will share a secret that Emeril never revealed to her. This secret will not only increase her feelings of betrayal. It may also place a target on her back that could ruin her and the company she's trying to save.

https://books2read.com/Queenofnorthshore

By birth, she is royalty. By choice she is an avenger and equalizer for those who have no voice. When dark forces emerge and threaten not only her queendom but her life, Luiza, Queen of Belize becomes a foot soldier, calling upon the assistance of allies and a few nemeses to help aid in a personal war. It's then that she fulfills the meaning of her name, glorious war hero.

https://books2read.com/Queenofbahia

Samantha DaCosta, reporter extraordinaire, stumbles upon an explosive story in her research of several wealthy, humanitarians connected to The Castle, a place reserved for the mega-rich.

Her uncle, who is a member, has invested in a medical facility that produces and distributes vaccines to third-world countries. The medication has deadly adverse effects, which sets up Ted DaCosta as a target for blackmail.

As Sam uncovers disturbing details, she's conflicted. When her personal safety is threatened, she must either pretend not to know the implications of this nefarious plot, or speak up and bring down a hailstorm of publicity. Danger also stalks her to Jamaica in the form of an assassination attempt.

Kingston "King" Coburn is content to support his woman's endeavors, but when work impacts her well-being, he draws the line. Instead of pulling her back from the edge of a dark abyss, he's drawn into the world of power brokers, who will do anything to increase their wealth.

Only the couple's combined skills and access to a safe haven will keep them alive at the end of their harrowing search for the truth.
https://books2read.com/Queen-of-Kingston

QUEEN OF CAMBRIDGE

Billionaire chocolatier Caressa Sidaná is one of the most recognizable names in the confectionery industry, but she is looking to expand into other ventures.

She is shrewd and no-nonsense, but in her pursuit of business dominance, she has made some mistakes along the way, including the oft-clichéd misstep of mixing business with pleasure.

Her expansion efforts lead to a chance meeting with Ishmael Abdur-Hafiz, an international weapons dealer with the type of connections that could prove beneficial for all parties involved. Their intense attraction and mutual business pursuits draw the attention of a former lover-turned-enemy, intent on ruining everything she has built and permanently removing Ishmael from her life.

Can she find a way to deal with the consequences of her decisions and save her company from potential destruction?

https://books2read.com/Queen-of-Cambridge

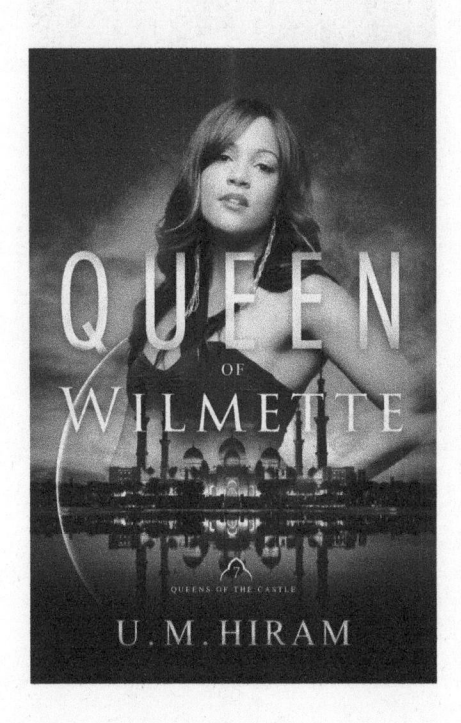

Milan Alessia Jackson battled through the scars left in her life from a contentious relationship. Her grandaunt served as her protector and guardian angel until she took her last breath. International lawyer Vikkas Germaine was her childhood friend and true love. Life's circumstances separated them, but his father served as the catalyst to reunite them.

As the couple settle into their new marriage and Durabia, unexpected challenges rise up and threaten to tear their relationship apart. Secrets from her past, an unexpected trip to South Carolina and family members primed to settle scores surface, leading to a whirlwind of upheaval in their lives. Can their love survive these storms or will forces in play destroy everything they're building?

https://books2read.com/QueenofWilmette

Waking up from a coma—without her memory intact—is not something Cassandra anticipated when she says her goodbyes to her best friend, promising to find her daughter, along with the other children who went missing since the arrival of an unknown criminal organization in Curaçao.

https://books2read.com/Queencuracao

Someone is tampering with the water supply in the small Brazilian community, causing many to get sick, including Pilár Silva's beloved grandmother. Pilár leaves Chicago and travels to Salvador, Bahia at the start of Carnival season. She must trust Yoshi Tanaka's expertise as a scientist and his abilities to keep her safe.

Yoshi, an award-winning Hydrologist, is supposed to stay in Rio for a conference, but he honors his brother's request to help a coworker from The Castle who's in the region. In order to keep Pilár safe, he must keep her close.

Danger stalks them like a thief in the night. Will they explore their budding feelings, or will one of them end up in a shallow grave?
https://books2read.com/Queenofbahia

ABOUT U. M. HIRAM

U.M. Hiram is a #1 Bestselling Author, Book Coach, and Interior Book Designer who currently resides in Kansas. She is also a human resource professional and 21-year retired Navy veteran writing in multi-genres that include Christian Fiction/Inspirational, Memoir, and Romance.

Her two latest releases are #1 Amazon Bestselling Persistence: The Power & Breakthrough of Fervent Prayer, Book #8 in the Merry Hearts Inspirational Book Series and Queen of Wilmette, Book #7 in the Queens of the Castle Series.

Reading, traveling, watching sports, and spending time with her family is what she enjoys doing the most when not putting pen to paper.

Website: https://authorumhiram.com/